P9-CCX-986

PUFFIN CANADA

SOMETHING WICKED

LESLEY ANNE COWAN was born in Toronto and studied English and education at McGill University in Montreal. She has travelled extensively and works as a secondary school teacher of at-risk youth. Her first novel, *As She Grows*, first published as adult literary fiction, was shortlisted for the Chapters/ Robertson Davies First Novel Prize. *Something Wicked* is the second in a series of adolescent novels exploring the lives of today's young, urban women.

Visit the author's website at www.lesleyanne cowan.com.

ALSO BY LESLEY ANNE COWAN

As She Grows

LESLEY ANNE COWAN

Something Wicked

PUFFIN
CANADA

PUFFIN CANADA

Published by the Penguin Group

Penguin Group (Canada), 90 Eglinton Avenue East, Suite 700, Toronto, Ontario, Canada M4P 2Y3 (a
division of Pearson Canada Inc.)

Penguin Group (USA) Inc., 375 Hudson Street, New York, New York 10014, U.S.A.
Penguin Books Ltd, 80 Strand, London WC2R 0RL, England
Penguin Ireland, 25 St Stephen's Green, Dublin 2, Ireland (a division of Penguin Books Ltd)
Penguin Group (Australia), 250 Camberwell Road, Camberwell, Victoria 3124, Australia
(a division of Pearson Australia Group Pty Ltd)
Penguin Books India Pvt Ltd, 11 Community Centre, Panchsheel Park, New Delhi – 110 017, India
Penguin Group (NZ), 67 Apollo Drive, Rosedale, North Shore 0632, New Zealand
(a division of Pearson New Zealand Ltd)
Penguin Books (South Africa) (Pty) Ltd, 24 Sturdee Avenue, Rosebank,
Johannesburg 2196, South Africa

Penguin Books Ltd, Registered Offices: 80 Strand, London WC2R 0RL, England

First published 2010

1 2 3 4 5 6 7 8 9 10   (WEB)

Copyright © Lesley Anne Cowan, 2010

Author representation: Westwood Creative Artists
94 Harbord Street, Toronto, Ontario M5S 1G6

ONTARIO ARTS COUNCIL
CONSEIL DES ARTS DE L'ONTARIO

All rights reserved. Without limiting the rights under copyright reserved above, no part of this
publication may be reproduced, stored in or introduced into a retrieval system, or transmitted in any
form or by any means (electronic, mechanical, photocopying, recording or otherwise), without the
prior written permission of both the copyright owner and the above publisher of this book.

Publisher's note: This book is a work of fiction. Names, characters, places and incidents either
are the product of the author's imagination or are used fictitiously, and any resemblance to actual persons
living or dead, events, or locales is entirely coincidental.

Manufactured in Canada.

LIBRARY AND ARCHIVES CANADA CATALOGUING IN PUBLICATION

Cowan, Lesley Anne
Something wicked / Lesley Anne Cowan.

ISBN 978-0-14-317393-9

I. Title.

PS8555.O85763S66 2010   C813'.6   C2010-901982-2

Visit the author's website at www.lesleyannecowan.com
Visit the Penguin Group (Canada) website at www.penguin.ca

Special and corporate bulk purchase rates available; please see
www.penguin.ca/corporatesales or call 1-800-810-3104, ext. 2477 or 2474

To those I've taught,
and those who've taught me

One

I am "sexually promiscuous."

The words are written down in my file. I can't escape it. It goes along with all my other labels: ADD, learning disability, irritability, and impulsivity. Once someone writes a label down, it's like a big fat bread crumb leading the counsellor down the care and treatment plan. You see, it's the person who holds the pen who matters; this is who can ruin your life. The one who takes every mistake you've made and every blurted-out word and etches it into your future with the stroke of a pen. Of course, the past shapes everyone's future, but with counsellors, the past *is* the future. The past is never, ever forgotten. You are forced to live it every day. And soon, it becomes who you are.

"Sexually promiscuous," I slowly read aloud, staring at the opened file on the table. "That's a new one. So you're saying I'm a slut?"

Eric, my counsellor, quickly covers up the papers. "No. It means you are perhaps more liberal in your sexual relations than adults feel is appropriate for your age group."

"So?" I challenge. "Does it matter?"

"It can."

"Well. It doesn't make a difference to me. Sex is not a big deal. It doesn't damage me or anything."

Eric shrugs and raises a brow, the way he does when I say something loaded and he's thinking whether or not to get into it with me. He knows, if it's the wrong time, I'll just argue and not listen, so he waits, like a predator in the grass, for a vulnerable moment when his attack is more likely to yield a good kill.

"I know the difference between fucking around and love," I add, because I don't want him thinking I'm a *total* idiot.

"I hope you do," Eric says casually.

I eye him with suspicion. I have slipped up. I shouldn't be telling him about all the guys I'm with. Even though he's a good counsellor, he's still from an old generation of people who think sex matters. It's just not a big deal anymore, and so I've divulged too much, as usual. Old habits die young. That's why teenagers are so exciting in therapy. We haven't yet learned that you aren't supposed to confess everything. We don't know that there are two languages: the one you keep in your head and the other you share with everyone else.

If you only knew. If you only really knew the truth about what I really do, I think, moving my gaze to the fishbowl. "So you still want me to name it?" I ask, trying to change the topic before he uses it as a window to further discussion. Eric has a goldfish that he always offers his clients to name. He pretends it's the same one, but from time to time I notice a slight change—a different brownish mark on the belly, a slightly thinner fin. It's been almost a year, and I've refused to do it.

"Sure."

I reconsider. "But isn't it a little schizophrenic for the little thing, all those names? It's a good thing you're a shrink."

Eric raises his hand to his reddish beard and pulls at the short hairs on his chin. "I'm not a psychiatrist. I'm a counsellor," he corrects me. He is so serious sometimes. "So, any ideas?"

"No." I lie, not wanting to give him the satisfaction. But I know exactly what I'd call it. And I actually don't think having more than one name is such a bad idea.

I have more than one name for myself. I also call myself Echo. It's sort of like a tag name, but I use it only for adults. I always like to introduce myself to strangers as this. Some of them stare at me like they know I'm bullshitting, but most either don't care or are too self-absorbed to care, and just don't question the name.

Eric has a hard time calling me this, though. I don't think he's ever said it, despite my insistence. So I'm not about to name his stupid fish. But if I did, I'd call her Amphitrite, because she was the goddess queen of the sea.

I am into myths. We study them in English class and my mother gave me a book on them last Christmas. It's the only book she's ever given me, despite the fact I love reading. She says myths contain more wisdom than the Bible, and more insight than a *Dr. Phil* episode. I just like them because the women sometimes kick ass and there's tons of crazy, heartless jealousy and revenge. Everybody is sleeping with everybody else. It's completely insane.

I liked Echo right away. She was a sleazy, beautiful nymph who tried to steal the goddess Hera's husband. Instead of getting mad at her man, the goddess put a stop to the flirting by cursing Echo to just repeat whatever a person said to her. She would have only the power of reply, no power to speak first. No original thought. So after that, her conversations with the guy went something like this:

"Who's here?" he asks.

"Here."

"Why do you shun me?" he asks.

"Shun me."

But this is where I'm torn. Though I identify with Echo, I have respect for Hera. She recognized the slut's true charm and instead of making her ugly, she took away her ability to flirt. That goddess was smart. And I'd like to think I'm pretty smart like that too. Not school smart. People smart. Most women would have mistakenly gone straight to the beauty factor. But we all know it's those ugly women who can pose the most threat.

You see? It's all about the words. Words control your destiny. Not just the ones etched on paper. Even the fleeting words in your mouth stain the air with deceptive permanence.

So I call myself Echo to remind me not to give away too much of myself when I talk to adults: repeat what they say. Say what they want to hear.

Eric trips me up sometimes. It's especially hard to be Echo with him. In fact, it's hard to remember most of the time, which is why I write this name on my library card, sign it on school papers, throw it into conversations. I want to make it obvious to adults that I get it, that I am now in the game: think what you want of me, you'll never get inside.

"Are you okay?"

"I'm okay."

"Everything all right?"

"All right."

But it's not just the *words* I repeat. It's not that literal. I replicate the *tone*. I use the same thought censorship that adults do. I've learned what shouldn't be divulged. I've learned to make the space between the words not impenetrable, but empty. So that when they try to dissect me, all they find is a void.

Two

Only two weeks since the beginning of the school year and already I'm tired of it. Is there a rule somewhere that school must be boring? That it must be irrelevant? That it must suck the life out of learning? You go into grade one all enthusiastic and curious, but by the time you graduate, you're shrivelled and dried like a dead lizard carcass you find behind the fridge.

Even this is not an original thought. Millions of teenagers believe school is boring. Even the teachers think it. Books have been written. Songs have been sung. It's so cliché.

So why does it continue?

"Tonight's homework will be worth five percent of your final mark."

Ms. Switzer's voice snaps me out of my daydream rant. My mind is pretty wild. Sometimes it just goes to places so far away that even *I* don't realize it's taken off until something jars me back to the present. That's my ADD. It takes me a moment to regain my bearings. Here I am, inside my stupid grade-eleven body, inside my stupid school uniform, inside a stupid English classroom, inside a stupid rundown high school, inside a pretty decent city, inside a pretty decent country, inside a stupid fucked-up world, inside a pretty cool universe.

Ms. Switzer's hand goes up and she scribbles our essay topic across the blackboard. Occasionally you get a good teacher like Ms. Switzer who makes you actually wake up out of your dazed stupor and learn something. She's not young or old, ugly or pretty. She's not a bitch or a softie. She's something in the middle of all those things, which just makes her … real.

She writes, *The first human statement is a scream.*

I am excited to do this assignment. I have so much to say. Great ideas race through my mind, but by the time I place my hand on the page, my head is already empty again. That's my learning disability: I can't squeeze my brilliant, billowing thoughts through my teeny, tiny pen and into sentences on a page.

⌒

The excitement over the English homework never went away, it's just that I get caught up in other things. Like after school, meeting my best friends Allison and Jessica, who beg me to come smoke a few blunts in the park because I've barely seen them all summer since I'm always with Michael. I met Ally in the beginning of grade nine, but Jess has been my friend since grade one. They're a lot different. Allison is tough and butchy, with steel-toed black combats, while Jessica is more like a plain-Jane princess with a sharp stick. But we all get along really good, especially when we're high.

Mark, Luc, Devon, and Kyle and a few other guys come along, stopping for some tokes before going to play hoops. We chill with them because Devon and Jess have been together forever, at least eight months. And Luc bought a twenty-sixer, and this Afro-haired guy who is hilarious had some E for us. And it is an Indian summer, and sitting with the grass tickling my bare legs, talking to Jess and Ally, checking out the guys, is just so … summer. And the ball slap-slaps against the hot asphalt and the metal chain net chink-chinks like shattering crystal, as if every sound were amplified a million times in my ear. And all this just overrides any recollection of English homework, because being here, now, is all that seems to matter. Life isn't in a classroom. This is where you find living. In this school field. In Jess's uncontrollable laughter. In Kyle's hand that picks at the grass and drops the shiny blades into piles on my bare legs. In his warm fingers rubbing the pieces off my thighs. In the smell of green.

Three

It's after nine when I leave the park, and the closer I get to my apartment, the more mad I become. It happens every day lately, no matter how good my day is. But this is nothing that new, because I'm so goddamn angry all the time. I don't know why. It's like I'm always on the edge. The only time I'm not angry is when I'm high. That's the only time I'm nice to people and it's the only time I feel like I'm a "nice person."

My mother says I was born with a scowl on my face, a permanently curled lip. She thinks that even when I was in the womb, I had my arms crossed the way I always do now. She says she could feel my pointy elbows through her tummy, like I was refusing to co-operate even in there. "I mean, what could you possibly be defying in the womb, Hon?"

She was only half joking when she said this, so I ignored her. I ignore most of what my mother says. She's not terrible or anything, she's just not the sharpest knife in the drawer, and most of what she says is stupid.

I'm hoping my mom won't be home, but I see her as soon as I open the door. She's lying on the couch in a tank and underwear, smoking a cigarette and watching her stupid soap opera. I throw my backpack on the chair and head to the kitchen to get something to eat.

"Well hello to you too!" she shouts.

I ignore her because I'm too focused on finding something, anything, other than potato chips and cereal to eat. I look in the cupboards and there's only canned peas and other canned shit. Then I look in the fridge. Nothing. Some pop, some mustard and other bottles, and a package of expired bacon.

"There's nothing to eat!"

"What do you mean? There's lots. Have some cereal."

I come out of the kitchen and pick up my backpack. "I'm fucking sick of that bran crap."

"Sorry, Hon, I'll order pizza," she says, not taking her eyes off the screen.

"It's too late. I'm going to bed."

"Where were you, anyway?" she asks, but I ignore her.

I slam the door to my room to show my disapproval of her mothering skills. I mean, she's supposed to provide, at the most basic, food and shelter. Isn't she? I take out my binder and lie in bed to start my English assignment.

The first human statement is a scream.

I pick up my pen and wonder where to start, what word to write first. I have so many thoughts. I think it's so true. That we're born into suffering. That we're these innocent little beings and that, as soon as we see the world, we take that first breath and scream 'cause we know life is going to be rough. I think about all the tragedies on the news and the crazy people and the wars happening. It's like sometimes I think humans were put on this earth as a test to see how much pain we can take.

After a while of still staring at the page, there's a knock on my door. "Hon?"

"I'm busy!" I shout.

She opens the door and pokes her head inside. She has makeup on and the perfume stench gushes into my room. "I'm heading out for a bit, okay? Won't be late, but don't chain the door."

"What about the pizza?"

"You said you didn't want any."

"Huggghh." I sigh loudly. "I would have had some. I'm still awake."

"Sorry," she says. "Look, I gotta go. Night night. Okay?" She winks and doesn't bother waiting for an answer.

I try to go back to my assignment, but now my mind is on my mom and too pissed off to think clearly, so I decide to just turn off the light and go to sleep and wake up early in the morning to finish it.

What is it about mothers that screws you up? Why can't the story ever be about fathers? Is it because they're always absent? My friends who actually know their messed-up fathers fall into seven categories: A) The father abuses the mother. B) The father abuses them. C) The father is an asshole. D) The father is a lazy ass. E) The father drinks. F) The father took off. G) All of the above.

All this is so overt. So easy to detect.

And my father? Trick question. Everything but B. So if this was on a test, I wouldn't be able to answer. Anyway, my father split when I was just a baby, so there is not much more I know about him (or care to know) other than he slept till noon, he was always late, when he spilled something he didn't clean it up, and he threw temper tantrums every once in a while. I know this because when I do all these things, my mother will say, "You're just like your father."

Mothers don't fit into these simple categories. They are more complicated. They screw you up without you even knowing it. At least with fathers, there's a definite conflict. A clear and present danger. And, hopefully, a clear resolution. Call the police. Call Children's Aid Society. Leave.

My mother.

Youngish. Hippish. Pretty.

Had a controlling father who wouldn't let her go to parties until she was eighteen.

And so she gave me independence at a young age. Instilled decision making. Discussed the rights and wrongs after the first time I trashed my room, at age ten, instead of punishing me. When I was fourteen, she took me to the gynecologist, who inserted a birth control capsule into my arm even though I wasn't yet having sex. Since I was smoking ganja anyway, she showed me how to responsibly roll a joint and measure amounts. And since I was partying, she let my friends and me party under her roof because it was safer than on the streets.

But she forgot something.

I'm a kid!

My brain is different. There are articles in science magazines about this. I highlighted the points and gave them to her.

Do as I say, not as I do.

Everyone knows this one too.

My mother.

Insecure. Addictive personality. Afraid of conflict.

Had a controlling father who wouldn't let her go to parties until she was eighteen. Then at eighteen and a half, she moved in with a boyfriend. At eighteen and nine months, she had me. At twenty-one, she had a second boyfriend, who had a small grow op in the back room beside my nursery. At twenty-two, she went into therapy and took medication. At twenty-three, she joined AA. At twenty-four, she went back to school until she got pregnant again with my little brother Bradley, who died when he was six. And then things *really* got messed up.

Four

Early the next morning, before school starts, I sit in the cafeteria with this guy in grade twelve, Jeremy, and have a coffee. Jeremy is a player, and all the girls both hate him and love him. He's so incredibly gorgeous and smart, he can do whatever he wants. Him and me are just friends, but we used to fool around every once in a while, just for fun.

We sit and talk about nothing special. I have my English homework in front of me: a blank page. I have been tapping my pen over it for fifteen minutes now, as if the ink would magically spill out and write the composition itself.

"I can write it right now for you," Jeremy finally offers. "Give me your pen."

I pass him my pen and paper.

"But it'll cost you," he adds, smiling slyly and running his tongue along his lip in this totally sexy way.

I roll my eyes. "Give me my pen back," I order, holding out my hand.

He pulls the pen away and holds it to his chest. "Why? What's wrong?"

"Just give it back," I say again, smiling but resolute. There's no way I will mess around with him now, because I have a boyfriend and I don't do that anymore. I don't blame him for trying, though, because nobody knows about me and Michael.

He passes me the pen and I put it down to the paper as if I'm going to write something. "Now, shut up. I need to concentrate," I say.

He gets up quickly, pushing the chair hard, making a high-pitched shrieking noise. I'm surprised he's so angry. It was no big deal, but whatever. I don't care. I keep my eyes on the page and he walks away.

For some reason I attract the most messed-up guys. I'm like a magnet for psychos—the ones with anger problems or jealousy or a few who seem incapable of caring deeply about anyone, including their families.

I wish every guy came with a description card disclosing his inner emotional baggage. Like those papers you get in a chocolate box telling you what's inside so you don't waste your efforts on something you know you won't like.

That's why, when I first met Michael, he seemed so totally normal that he was almost boring. It's like I bit into him, expecting something to come oozing out, but all there was was a little dribble of depression and an ex-girlfriend.

During the first few weeks, I didn't know how to handle it. Without the usual constant fighting I have with a guy, the flatlined calm made me feel like he wasn't really into me. I kept trying to pick a fight about the smallest things, but he didn't bite. At least when you fight, you get a sign that a guy cares about you. But then Michael explained it to me one day. He told me it's like I have to learn a different language of love. "It's called words and expression," he said.

The thing about Michael is that he's twenty-eight. We were just friends for almost a year, but we got together about three months ago, just after I turned sixteen. People think a sixteen-year-old girl can't really love. A man, that is. And definitely not a twenty-eight-year-old man. Sure, a sixteen-year-old can love a pet or an actor or a favourite pair of jeans. She can love a parent, a sibling, even a hamster. All of these kinds of love are clearly legitimate. But any feeling toward a man is considered a childish crush. It's something cute or trivial, somehow not as legitimate as adult love. And a sixteen-year-old loving a man? This is inconceivable. But I'm living proof: it can happen.

Five

Because it's Jess's birthday, she, Mya, Shayla, and I decide to chill out behind the equipment hut by the school's back parking lot during third period. We're so high that none of us notice our vice-principal, Ms. Brentworth, turn the corner until it's too late.

What can we do? Blunts in our mouths. Smoke in the air. We're busted.

The four of us trudge down the hallway behind Ms. Brentworth, who walks like a pig on tippy-hooves, her fat calves and bulging feet stuffed into her tiny black shoes. When we pass a garbage bin, I'm quick to toss in my stash of weed, even though it kills me to lose it all. Someone immediately taunts, "Yo, Mel, what's up?" and I know it'll be gone when I come back.

We are taken into the office and Jessica and Mya are allowed to go home after a little blah blah blah, but since Shayla and I were the ones holding the joints, we have to wait three hours for our parents to show up. This will be my fifth high school suspension. Four were for skipping and one for "persistent opposition to authority," when I refused to leave the classroom last year because I wasn't going to blindly obey a teacher who was a male chauvinist pig.

My mom doesn't even look at me when she arrives. She just goes straight to the counter and asks for Ms. Brentworth. Then she sits on one of the chairs closest to the door and starts rummaging through her purse. When Shayla's mom arrives, she goes right up to Shayla and speaks through gritted teeth. "This is it, Shayla. This is it!" I know she'll be in a lot of trouble, mostly from her father. Her mother is just the warm-up. Her parents used to live in rural India, and life is just entirely different there for girls. Shayla says they think she is the Devil sometimes.

"Whoa," I tease when her mom walks away. "You're in shit."

"Shut up," Shayla replies, punching me in the arm.

Our two mothers sit beside each other. They look so different. Shayla's mom is in a business suit, with the blazer folded on her lap. My mom is wearing a jean jacket and thick-soled flip-flops. Her nails are painted pink with swirly butterfly designs on both big toes. My friends think I'm lucky to have such a cool mom, but they don't have to live with her. Sometimes I'm proud how beautiful and young she looks. People always question my mom about her being a model, and then they look at me and shut their mouths because I'm just average pretty. She used to try to get me to wear feminine, tight clothes like her, but we just don't have the same body. And most of the time I find her taste tacky anyway, a cross between that bold, gold Québécois jewellery and Brazilian bling.

⟿

"They were all smoking marijuana," Ms. Brentworth explains to our moms when we are finally called into her office.

"You mean each girl had a joint in her hand?" Suddenly my mother's mood has changed. It seems she is no longer mad at me. It seems she's now pissed off at Ms. Brentworth. I want her to shut up. Shayla's mom isn't saying a thing. She just sits in her chair like a normal parent, looking humiliated and furious.

"No. Actually. Only Melissa and Shayla had the joints in their hands. That's part of the reason why they are here now and the other girls were sent home."

My mom darts me a disappointed look. Not because I had the joint in my hand but because I ruined her plan of attack. "And the other part of the reason?"

"I'm sorry?"

"You said that's part of the reason," my mother persists. Why is she being so confrontational?

Ms. Brentworth opens her desk drawer and removes a plastic bag full of a few hundred empty dime bags.

"What's that?" Shayla's mom asks.

"Well. It's a few hundred Baggies, suggestive of trafficking purposes."

"You had that?" Shayla's mom turns to her. "What are you doing with that? You selling drugs? Is that what you're doing when you're out at night? Is that what's been happening right outside my home, in the park?" Her mom really lays into her. Shayla keeps her head down, I'm sure humiliated that I'm witnessing the public lynching.

"Ms. Jaya ..." Brentworth interrupts. "We don't think Shayla and Melissa are drug dealers. But we do wonder why they had this paraphernalia in their possession. We also are extremely concerned about the amount of marijuana brought onto school property. We have discretionary expulsion and notification of police in matters of trafficking. But since we haven't caught the girls in the act of selling, we're going to suspend them for five days for being under the influence of illegal drugs on school property. We are also going to suspend them for another five days for possessing illegal drugs."

"Ten days? What good is keeping them out of school for ten days going to do?" my mom pipes in. "Guess what they'll do during that time? Because it ain't gonna be school work."

"Please understand, Ms. Sullivan. We need to ensure our school is a safe place for all attending students. It is highly concerning to have students bringing drugs onto school property, and using them. We have an obligation to terminate the behaviour. Sometimes it's necessary to involve the police."

"For a little bag of weed?" My mother laughs. "Come on, Ms. Brentworth. We all experimented when we were young —"

I bury my head in my hand. What is she doing? *Shut up! Shut up! Shut up!*

"But we know Shayla and Melissa have the potential to be positive peer influences," Ms. Brentworth masterfully interjects, shutting my mom right up. "They both have good leadership potential, if channelled in the right direction."

⌒

We listen to the radio on the car ride home. My mom seems pretty happy. She doesn't ask me about the drugs — whose they were or what we were going to do with them. Then, at a stoplight, she turns down the radio and I prepare myself for the lecture. "Listen. I know you smoke sometimes, Melissa. But don't be an idiot about it. Don't do it on school property. And not during school hours. Okay?"

"Okay."

Done. Easy.

The radio goes back on and I turn to the window, relieved she isn't going to make a big deal about it. I have bigger things to worry about than my mother being mad at me. Freestyle will kill me for getting busted and losing the weed, even if he is my uncle. I owe him a lot of money now since I can't sell it, so I'll have to pick up extra shifts during my suspension to pay him back.

"She said you have leadership potential," my mom comments when we pull into the underground garage.

"What?" I ask, distracted. My mind is still focused on my plans to pay back Freestyle.

"Your vice-principal said you have leadership potential," she repeats with a smile, like she's all proud of me.

"Oh," I answer. Maybe coming from a normal parent this compliment would be nice, but I just can't help but be annoyed that she has found a way to make my suspension a positive thing.

Six

My boyfriend, Michael, thinks I have potential too. He gets really upset when I tell him two nights later about the suspension. He thinks I'm better than that and it's my bad choice in friends that is holding me back.

After I explain what happened, Michael sits me down across from him at his kitchen table and tells me I have to make a ten-year plan. Sometimes he acts like he's my father that way, all protective and serious. We go over how many school credits I need to graduate. We look at the university requirements for veterinary college. He even says he'll call to make an appointment for a campus tour. He makes me write down my entire school timetable and commit to a final grade for each course. As I'm doing his "assignment," I start to feel excited about my future. I can actually do this! Actually, since I met him, I feel like I can almost do anything.

A thought occurs to me. I put down my pen and look at him. "What about your ten-year plan?"

"I did it ten years ago."

"Did it work?"

"No," he says. "Unfortunately, life gets in the way of those plans sometimes."

And he doesn't have to explain. I know he's talking about his depression. He's already told me about being a keener university student who had it all—the perfect girlfriend, perfect grades, perfect family. And when depression hit him, it knocked him completely off his feet, because it was like the first obstacle that ever stood in his way. He said he just stood there, stunned, staring at this ugly monster that jumped onto his path, and he froze in fear.

"So then, why am I doing it if it doesn't work?" I ask.

"Because sometimes life doesn't get in the way," he says with regret, as if there's still hope for me but it's all over for him. It breaks my heart to see him so down. He isn't that bad. I know some people would think he's a loser to be with a sixteen-year-old. They'd think he has some kind of problem and can't get a girl his own age. But other than being a little quiet and boring, he's totally normal.

I get up out of my chair, lean far across the table on my elbows, and kiss him hard. Then I crawl up over the table all sexy, like I'm in a music video, finagle my way down onto his chair, and straddle his lap, all the while kissing. I'm still wearing my school uniform—I know it's something Michael just can't resist.

After fooling around all over the kitchen, we end up lying on the bed just holding each other, naked only down to our waists. I rest my head on top of his heart and fan my hair out over his chest. His arms tightly wrap around me, not hairless and scentless boyish arms but real man's arms. And I'm not thinking about my bad breath or getting high or about what to say. Instead, we just are. I just am. And my life is perfect.

I don't know why he makes me so happy. We don't do much. Sometimes we drive to the mall. Not the closest one—too many people he might bump into there. Sometimes we go to movies or have breakfast at this diner in the east end. But usually we are in his apartment, watching TV or making dinner or just reading. This is where our relationship lives. Inside these four walls.

"Why are you with me?" I ask him. It is something I've always wanted to know since we've been together, but was afraid that if I asked he actually might not be able to come up with a good reason.

"Because you make me feel good," he says right away. "You think everything I do is great."

"Hey!" I lift my head up to look into his eyes. "Me too. That's the same for me."

"And you're beautiful." He starts to run his hand through my hair.

I slap him on the chest. "No I'm not."

"Yes you are."

"How am I beautiful?"

"Well, let's see ..." He lifts his head to carefully look me over. "Of course, your face is beautiful. And your body. And your skin. Your smile." He lifts my hair up. "... Your ears."

"My ears?" I slap him again. I'm embarrassed to hear him talk like that. Deep down I just don't think it's true, 'cause I know my looks aren't amazing.

"Ahhhh!" he jokes, grabbing my hand. "Don't hurt me! I can't take any more pain in my life."

I pull my hand away, roll over onto my back. "Hmm." I don't really know what to say. I know he was sort of joking, but for the past while he's been telling me that he was feeling depressed. It feels strange to hear a guy admit he's unhappy, because all the other guys I know are just angry. And the fact that he's still unhappy makes me feel like I'm not good enough, because I should be making life perfect for him, the way he has done for me. Since I met Michael, it's as if all the bad things in my life don't exist anymore. Finally, God answered one of my prayers and gave me someone who loves me in a way no one has before. And I want to do the same for him. I want to be the answer to Michael's prayers.

"I wish I could make a time machine that would speed up time for you but keep it still for me and we could meet in ten years," he says. It drives him crazy that he's twelve years older than me, and for teenagers he thinks age is counted like dog years. One human year is the same as seven dog years. So that means he's basically eighty-four years older.

"Yeah? And who will I be then?" I ask, sitting up on my knees.

He spreads his big hands out over my head as if I were a crystal ball and starts rubbing his fingertips against my scalp. "I see a woman wearing a suit jacket and heels. I see someone who can stand in front of a roomful of businessmen and stun them with her assertiveness and brains."

By the time he finishes, my hair is tangled in knots. I reach out to do the same to his head, but then I pull away. "I better not," I joke, closely inspecting his receding hairline. "It might all fall out."

"Shut up," he says, playfully pushing me backward.

"Here, I'll be gentle." I become serious and replace my hands at his temple. I close my eyes and try to picture him ten years from now. Then I open my eyes again. "What will you be ... almost forty?"

"Hey—only thirty-eight."

"Same thing," I say. I try to envision forty and I see every old guy in my apartment building. I see Michael in a jogging suit, with a belly and a half-bald head. Then I see him eating a slice of pizza and holding a six-pack under his arm. "Forget it.

Nothing's coming to me. I can't do it." I drop my hands, feeling sad all of a sudden.

"That's a bad sign."

"Okay, let me try again." I replace my hands a third time, close my eyes, and really, really concentrate. I tell myself that Michael isn't like the men in my apartment building, and this time I like what I see. "You have a little less hair and a little bigger belly, but you're still good-looking. You are in the big backyard of our house by a little swing set. Our two little girls are playing with you. I am walking toward you, bringing out some cheese sandwiches cut into fours without the crusts."

"Nice," he says, and pulls me back down onto his chest. And I think it's the happiest moment in my life.

Seven

I go to my job at the veterinary clinic almost every day I'm suspended. My mom thought I'd sit around and smoke pot all day, but I'm actually excited to get up every morning and go to work. It's like I'm living my future adult life, and for once it's easy to get out of bed and start my day.

Rachel, the daytime co-op student from an uptown school, greets me right away. "Melissa!" She's just inside the door, as if she was waiting hours for my arrival. "Oh my God! You'll die! Penelope had her pups! They're adorable."

"Hey!" I am so excited I push past her and rush toward the basement, where the cages are. I am practically skipping down the stairs. "I was hoping it was today!"

"The black and white one is mine," she claims, chasing after me.

I suppose you could say Rachel and I are "friends." I started to volunteer at Willow Animal Hospital almost two years ago now. My school guidance counsellor set it up, and it's been the best thing that has ever happened to me. When I turned sixteen, they hired me on as part-time casual, and started me off on a higher wage because of all my previous help.

Rachel has been there for only a month, so basically she's my "student."

Rachel is a "normal" girl. She has two parents. She takes piano lessons. She's on the swim team. She drives a Mini. She's still a virgin. She seems a billion years younger than me. I think she's a little afraid of me. She's seen me not take crap from Tawyna, the dog groomer who thinks she can boss us around like slaves. But Rachel would never guess what I'm really like. The drugs. The parties. My mom. Because here at work, I am me. I don't have a mythic name. At work, I am Melissa.

⌒

The pups, all pink and squeaking, are intertwined in a writhing huddle in a blanket on the floor of the kennel. Their mother, Penelope, is in a separate cage, recovering from two broken legs.

"Look at them! They're soooo cute!" I open the kennel door and sit cross-legged on the concrete floor. I spend the next fifteen minutes holding each one, bringing their new-baby-smell bodies up to my face and giving them a thousand kisses. Rachel sits in the pen with me, doing the same thing.

I love my work. I want to be a veterinarian. This job will give me the experience I need to get into the university program. I work in the lab. I administer medication. I give animals needles. I assist in minor surgeries. If I stay on for a late shift, I even get to help with car accident victims or neutering.

For the most part, though, I'm downstairs taking care of the cats and dogs. Some of them are boarders, some surgery, some sick. When I arrive each day, Rachel gives me a rundown on the animals: which ones to walk, which ones need meds, which ones bite. We go by each cage and pretend we're interns giving medical summaries on each patient.

I start my shifts with walking the dogs on a little square patch of grass surrounding a single tree out behind the parking lot. It's not as easy as you'd think. Each dog has his own problem. Some have cones around their necks, or bandages around their legs, or even IV drips in their little doggy elbows. Some dogs, like the ones who have had hip surgery, I have to carry up and down the stairs. After walking, I clean the cat and dog cages and feed everyone. Then I bathe the ones who shit all over themselves. In between all this, I do loads and loads of laundry.

⤳

Another reason I love my work is because it's where I met Michael. He's an animal technician, which for the most part he thinks makes him a failure. He wanted to be a vet too, but because of his depression, a few years ago he dropped out of university.

I met him on a late shift. I was filling in for Christie, the overnight lady. Jetson, a terribly mangy cat, was brought in, its eyeball popping out of its head. Blood everywhere. Smashed-up teeth. Michael was the only medical staff there. The on-call vet was nowhere to be found because he was having an affair with the convenience store owner's daughter next door, so it was just the two of us, and we worked like a team from *ER* to bring this mess back to life. It was amazing. And at the end, after two hours, we were so damn proud of ourselves, we toasted apple juice to our brilliance. And to Jetson's speedy recovery.

The cat died the next day. But Michael and I became friends. I never even considered him a real guy at first, because I knew he was so much older. He was also too "plain" and conservative. Normally I would have never looked twice at him. He had boring short brown hair, boring clothes, and, with the exception of some faded freckles, a sort of nondescript face. He was average height, average build, and maybe even had a bit of a gut. But almost a year later, a bit before summer, it all just happened: Michael became sort of beautiful to me. And just over three months ago was the beginning and the end of me.

"Michael is going to want to take them all home," I say to Rachel, putting back one of the puppies. I try to say his name as much as I can at work, just to feel the shape of it in my mouth.

"For sure," she affirms, and I glance to see if there's any suspicion about our secret relationship. None. It's hard to keep love a secret. In some ways, I'm dying to tell someone about our relationship. For the longest time I've just been waiting for Rachel to ask that exact question—"Are you and Michael together?"—so that I don't have to really answer, so that just my look will give it away.

⟨⟩

With the exception of Jess and Ally, no one knows about Michael. Why complicate the situation by involving judgment from those who can't possibly understand? My mother will get protective. My guidance counsellor will get concerned. My other friends will get grossed out. And what's worse is I'll start to believe them. *Yeah, maybe he did use me. Yeah, maybe I am seeking a father figure. Yeah, maybe he is a loser who can't get girls his own age.*

And I'd start to put the fence back up around my heart and believe that I was taken advantage of. And what good would that do? It was Michael who took the fence down. Opened me raw. Made me feel ... something. Anything. He gave me that gift. And even if our relationship is wrong, even if his love turns out to be a lie, I want to keep it. I don't want to close up again.

Eight

I had a feeling something was wrong. Extra wrong. Michael had been acting strange the past few days. And tonight, he's real cranky and distant. I get a feeling he's about to break up with me or something. After about an hour of watching TV together on the couch, he finally says it. "I've been wanting to talk to you …"

I know instantly what he's going to say. During the entire three months we've been together, I've been a secret to Michael's friends. He said they would kill him if they knew what he was up to. Sometimes our age difference really gets to him and he gets all distant with me for a couple of days, but then it's like he can't help his feelings and he gets close again. He told me once he was ashamed about the whole thing. It was just wrong for a twenty-eight-year-old man to be with a sixteen-year-old girl, even if he was young at heart. Even if we didn't have sex. Even if we were mostly friends.

"First, I want to say that …" he goes on, "it's not you. It's society. And that's a whole lot bigger than two people in a room." He raises his hand to push the hair off my face and kisses my forehead, like he is my father or something.

"Fuck society." I flick his hand and move away from him

toward the corner of the couch.

"I can't. You can't. We live in it. I made that decision a long time ago, probably about your age. Either you live in it, or you complain about it your whole life, or you deceive yourself into believing you're going against it."

"Then fuck me," I whisper, moving back toward him and putting my hands firmly on his thighs.

"Hah!" He pushes away my grip. "I can't do that either."

I kick at the coffee table in front of us. "Then fuck this."

I am pissed off at his bullshit. He's a man. He should do what he feels like, not what society tells him. But I can tell by the look on his face that it's serious. That maybe he is really about to break up with me. And I just can't believe it. I feel like I need to walk away, before he actually comes out and says it.

I stand, pick up my jacket, and head down the narrow hallway toward the door. The departure is dramatic. I stomp my PUMA runners as hard as I can. My jacket zipper scratches against the wall.

"Melissa …" Michael's voice trails behind me. "Melissa …" His voice gets louder and more distressed, so I slow my grip on the apartment doorknob to give him a few seconds, that's all, the way I've seen my mom do it when she's fighting with a boyfriend and she's trying to turn things around. She makes them come after her, and somehow, miraculously, has them apologize for nothing they've done wrong.

I give Michael just a few seconds to reconsider, but there is a long silence and I know he's forcing himself to try to say the right thing, do the right thing, be the right thing.

"And fuck you!" I shout, open the door, and slam it behind me. I wait outside the door, listening for his footsteps coming down the hallway. I wait for a few minutes, my heart starting to race. I thought he would call me back in.

He was supposed to call me back in.

As soon as I get to the bus stop, I call Michael on my cell, but he doesn't answer. Then I call him again when I get home, but he still doesn't answer. I go to his apartment building early the next morning, but he doesn't come to the door even after I pound for like twenty minutes. I go outside the building and throw rocks up to his windows. Still nothing. Then I call and call and call all day from school, at least one hundred times. Nothing. I hate myself for getting so mad at him. For swearing and being so mean. I apologize over and over again in every email and text. Nothing.

Then, the next morning when I call his cell, it's not in service. I leave school and go straight to his apartment, but when I knock, it sounds empty and hollow inside. I pound on all the neighbours' doors until one old man opens his door just a crack, chain still on, and tells me that the man who lived in 7C moved today.

"Today? You sure?" I stare in his direction, but the opening is so small I can barely even see his face.

"Saw the boxes myself."

"Where did he go?"

"Now, that I don't know, little lady." He starts to close his door. "I mind my own business."

I walk away, down the corridor toward the stairwell. My head spins. My mouth gets dry. I stop and lean a hand up against the wall, 'cause I feel like I'll drop.

It's like my soul has left my body and I am a walking corpse. I just can't believe he's gone. Move? Just like that?

I go home, change my clothes, drink four shots of vodka

from the bottle stashed under my bed, and then go to Ally's house, who's there chilling with her friend Jasmyn, a skanky girl from Ally's friend's group home. I didn't really like Jasmyn, but I trust Ally's judgment and give her a chance.

As soon as I walk into the basement, Ally knows there's something wrong with me. "Watz up?" she asks.

Even almost sober, I can barely hold back the tears, so I just say, "I don't want to talk about it. Let's just get fucked up."

She's cool with that answer. Which is why she's such a good friend. Good friends are there when you need them and there when you tell them to fuck off too.

The night goes on forever. Actually, it goes on for three days. We go to Jasmyn's friend's apartment where these four guys in their twenties live, though I can't figure out which ones because it's a full-on party house and random people come and go the whole time. There are tons of drugs. Ally, Jasmyn, and I start out sitting close together on the ratty couch, feeling like we don't really belong, but then one guy hooks us up and things get going. I'm so upset about Michael that I just want to have fun and forget what happened for a while, so I put everything I'm offered into my mouth or up my nose: two lines of coke, six E's, five prescription Concertas, two vials of K, and God knows how much alcohol. I lose count. I'll try anything once. Pills. K. Meth. Coke. Morphine. E. Acid. Whatever. But I won't do some things twice. Like meth. That's like suicide a second time. One taste of heaven has to be enough. I've seen too many people screw up their lives from that shit.

Time passes. I don't know if it's day or night. The blinds are down the whole time and there's cardboard up against the other bare windows. I don't eat. All I do is sleep, wake up, do drugs, watch movies, sleep, make out, wake up, do drugs, stare at the TV screen. I'm so messed up I don't know what's happening. I open my eyes and find some guy kissing me, but I push him off 'cause his mouth is all wet and sloppy and stinky. Then I come to again and I'm in the washroom and a different guy has his hand up my top, but I'm too wasted to care. At some point, on the second night, Jasmyn disappears into the bedroom with two other guys for a few hours. Ally, who always seems sober no matter how much she takes, makes a scene and keeps knocking on the door to make sure she's okay.

"She keeps telling me to fuck off, but I'm not going to stop," Ally reports back to me. "She's totally messed up. She's an idiot to be in there with them alone. You know what kind of shit can happen?" She's going on and on about it and I nod my head to agree, though I don't care so much because I don't really know Jasmyn.

Then, totally randomly, while I'm dozing off on this guy's lap and Ally is watching TV, Jasmyn comes tearing out of the room. "Let's go! Let's go!"

Her voice is so loud and terrified that we don't hesitate to jump up and run out behind her. You don't need a long explanation when you've hung out with people like this before. You know there's bad shit. Guns. Drugs. Messed-up guys. So we just run, like it is our lives at stake.

When we get to the road, Jasmyn buckles over, laughing hysterically. Her slutty miniskirt is hiked up so high, we can see her thong underwear. "Mother fucka! That goddamn shit." She turns to us. "You know what he wanted? He wanted me to piss on him. You know? Like sit on his chest and piss. Golden shower? What da hell?"

Ally reaches out and pushes Jasmyn backward. "Fuck you! You terrified me. I thought it was something bad."

"Fuck you," Jasmyn retaliates, pushing back. "You don't think piss is bad?"

Ally kisses her teeth and continues walking down the road. She decides we should hide on the porch of a house because the guys might follow us since Jasmyn still has some of their weed. Ally's smart like that. She chooses a dark house with no cars in the driveway and three newspapers sitting outside the door.

"No one's home here," Ally concludes. "We'll chill here for a bit." She sits down on the battered-up couch on the front porch and we just follow her. I pop the last pill of whatever I have, that I found in my pocket. We smoke a few blunts and soon things are fine, we're laughing about stupid shit, until Jasmyn decides that she has to go pee and insists she needs a toilet.

"Just piss behind the bush," Ally says, still annoyed at her.

"Fuck that. I'm no dog. You calling me a bitch? That what you sayin'?" And it's like Jasmyn gets all psycho and Allison and I exchange looks like this girl is *really* fucked up. I mean, way more fucked up than me. So we know not to argue. Jasmyn's fake nails alone would scratch our eyes out. "I'm going inside," Jasmyn announces.

"What?" Ally asks.

"How?" I ask.

"I'm going through this motha-fuckin' front door," she declares, flicking off her high-heel shoe, hiking her miniskirt, and giving the door a big kick. "Shit!" she wails, buckling over in fake laughter. "Fuck this shit. I'm going around the back."

Ally and I keep talking, not too worried about what she's up to. We figure she'll have the same problem back there and will end up peeing in the yard anyway.

"What's her story?" I ask, even though I'm too high to truly care.

"She's cool. Really. She's nuts. But she's cool. I don't know. I like her. She'll watch your back. She's been through some crazy shit."

"I don't know …"

The front door opens. "Ladies, welcome to my home," Jasmyn announces in a bad British accent.

We are so stunned and it's all so crazy that we rush in and shut the door behind us.

"This is insane," Ally says as she turns on the hallway light.

"Don't turn on the light," Jasmyn shouts, and Ally immediately turns it back off.

It's my first time breaking in. It's creepy to be in a stranger's house. There is a distinct homey smell that's hard to describe, other than it just isn't yours. It looks like the people left in a hurry. There are open letters sprawled out across the kitchen table. A man's suit jacket is on the back of a chair. Some dirty dishes are in the kitchen sink.

It makes me think of when Crystal, my mom's friend, had her apartment broken into. She was all upset about the violation of her "spiritual refuge." She spent months trying to reclaim the energy of her personal possessions that the person stole from her just by snooping around. But the thing is, I realize now that when you're doing it, it's like you don't even think of the people as "people." I remember telling Crystal that the robbers are just looking for stuff to take, they don't stand there and contemplate the photographs or kids' toys. But she still called it a "rape of her space," which makes me feel now that maybe she was right in a way.

Jasmyn finds the stereo, blasts FLOW 93.5, and begins to dance in the living room. The windows vibrate. The last pill starts to hit me hard. I can't think straight. I start dancing. More like jumping up and down. I pretend I'm more high than I am, and I keep my eyes closed mostly because I don't want anything to do with stealing. I won't steal from a person. It's just not right. Stores are different. They make so much money, and they're not going to miss a shirt or eyeshadow. But stealing from a person is just hurtful. Unless they're a bitch or a jerk, in which case they might deserve it. And this family? They're probably away at a cottage or something, having a nice time, and they're gonna come home to find their stuff gone, and I just can't be a part of that.

A while later, the girls return from upstairs. Ally proudly shows me a fistful of jewellery and shoves it in her jacket pocket. Even though I didn't really steal anything myself, I'd be lying if I didn't say the rush feels good. It's like all of me is alive and tingling and breathing. We laugh and laugh and laugh while marching down the middle of the street, as if we owned the whole world. But it takes only a few seconds for the red flashing lights to appear behind us.

Jasmyn tries to run for it but falls over her ridiculous high-heeled shoes and does a face-plant on the pavement. Ally and I just stand there with bewildered looks on our faces. But then, when the police approach, I start to laugh. Hysterically. Laugh, laugh, laugh so hard it's not until I feel the heat between my legs and the wet between my toes that I realize I've pissed my pants. And then I laugh even harder, because life is such a joke. Reality has a way of slapping you in the face over and over and over again, like it's waking you up from the stupid dream that had you believing your life was actually going to get better. And somehow the predictability of that disappointment, those flashing red lights, the fact that you totally knew the defeat was coming, is just so funny.

Nine

I always stand a moment or two outside the front door to our shitty little apartment, on our shitty little street, in our even shittier neighbourhood. I stand there as if I'm trying to decide whether or not to enter. As if I have a choice. As if I am ever brave enough to just turn and run.

But I do it anyway. Stand a moment or two. Fantasizing about the possibility.

When I open the door, I step into another world. In this world, I am not Echo. In this world, I am Syphilis. Okay, that's not his real name. I call him that to make myself laugh. His real name is Sisyphus. He showed a lack of respect for the gods, and pretty much any authority. Because of this, he was cursed by Zeus and doomed to forever roll a huge, heavy boulder up a hill. I mean *forever*. When he got to the top, instead of rejoicing in his achievement, or sitting down for a rest, he had to immediately roll the rock back down and then heave it up the hill again. It never stopped. He never finished his task. For all eternity.

To me, the tragedy isn't that he was doomed to labour up and down this crappy hill. It's that he got no false hope along the way.

False hope is a blessing. It keeps us alive.

And so, when I open the door to my apartment, I'm Syphilis.

⸺

Sometimes a door is just a door. Other times a door is the partition between two things. Like a past and a future. A good choice and a mistake. Your life now and your life after. Thing is, with a door, you pretty much have to walk through it. You pretty much don't have a choice. You could walk on by, but that's useless if the intent is to get to the other side.

When I open the door, on the other side is the rest of my life. In the living room, seated around a surprisingly clean coffee table, is my Children's Aid Society social worker, my probation officer, my mother, and her hippie flower child best friend, Crystal. It's been two days since the cops brought me home in the cruiser that night, waking my mom up, explaining to her that they found me with two girls who had stolen goods in their possession. They had taken Jasmyn and Ally to the detention centre, but charged me with break and enter and drove me home since I didn't have anything on me.

"Melissa?"

Which one said it? Lately, all four of their voices have blurred into one. And even though I've sobered up, I'm still dopey after those days of partying.

My heart races.

Turn and run. Turn and run. Turn and run.

"We need to talk to you."

And so, just like that, I am moving into a group home. My mother can no longer control my behaviour. It is dangerous to have a sixteen-year-old girl AWOL all weekend, spending nights in strange guys' apartments, doing drugs, and exposing herself to other potentially harmful experiences. And since my break and enter charge and my school suspension, there seems to be no hope left for me.

"Is this about something else?" I ask suspiciously.

"About what?" Sue, my CAS social worker, asks, her head cocked like a hawk hearing the faint squeak of a mouse miles away. "A charge? A suspension? What else could there possibly be?"

I figure they must know about Michael. A twenty-eight-year-old boyfriend can't be kept a secret forever, even if it is legal since I turned sixteen. Jessica must have blabbed at some point. Or perhaps they read my journal. The discovery would be just cause for panic, even if we did just break up.

"Is there something you should tell us?" Sue persists.

Relief. They don't know. "No."

"We gave you lots of warnings, Melissa," says Julie, the probation officer, a youngish woman who barely knows me. "You knew this was coming."

They are right about that. Syphilis knew it was coming. So she kept doing what she always did. Rolling the rock.

Up. Up. Up.

She kept rolling because she was cursed to do this forever. And hope? That after this crest there will be relief? Life will be better? She would be happy? Why attempt to change when you know the next step is just to roll the rock back up again?

"Yeah ... I knew it was coming," Echo repeats. I look at my mother, who sits with her head buried under her hands. She can't even look me in the eye. Truth is, I want to go. I don't want to live here anymore. I don't want to deal with my mother's bullshit boyfriends and mood problems. I want my own life. And really, what can I do? Ask to leave my mother? Ask someone to stop her from destroying my life? You can't ask for that without a gut-wrenching knife ripping open your soul, the guilt oozing out, the stain of mother abandonment forever on your skin. I don't want to be like psycho Lady Macbeth, wringing her hands and mumbling to herself in dark corners, for the rest of my life.

No. You can't ask to leave your mother. It must be forced upon you.

You must be taken away kicking and screaming.

But then my mom starts to weep. And even the stupid CAS worker's eyes well up. And so, in the end, I don't have to go to a group home, because my mother says she'll enforce a curfew. I sign a bullshit contract stating I'll obey. And then we all sit and have coffee. And they talk about me, around me, with these grandiose plans. And I stare in disbelief into the newly polished coffee table, watching our morphed reflections — the stretched mouths, the pinched heads, like sci-fi creatures speaking a fantasy language. What just happened?

"Your court date for the B and E is three months away," my probation officer says. "That gives you time to turn things around. They will be looking for a big change, especially considering your school suspension last week. It doesn't look good, Melissa, I'll be frank with you. You'll need to go to school, stop AWOLing all weekend. And you'll need to see your counsellor every week."

"There's a great school I've referred other young women to. You could be in there within two weeks. It's a small classroom with a nice teacher and youth workers who can help you. It will look good to the judge if you show them you're getting treatment," my CAS worker adds.

"Treatment? For what? What treatment?"

"Attending school. Coping skills for stress. Drugs. Harm reduction. They help you with all that."

"I'll try to get some time off work to spend some quality time together," my mother says.

"Ha!" I laugh. "Like that will ever happen." It takes me a second to realize I must have thought that aloud, 'cause I look up and everyone is staring at me. I can't help it. I'm pissed off. What a fucking joke. Gimme a break. Who are these people kidding? All their stupid plans. Always plans to fix things when they can't be fixed. How can adults be so fucking naive? Of course I'm messed up. Look at my mother. Lives off the men she dates. Can't keep a job. Doesn't buy food half the time. Of course I need out of here. I feel the red in my face burn, burn, burn. My knees start bouncing up and down, my jaw clenches, and my mouth gets tiny tight. Why can't someone have the balls to pull the plug when the tub is obviously overflowing? When I'm drowning, getting sucked down into a shit life? Stupid. Stupid. Stupid. I shake my head at the whole pathetic scene, tightly cross my arms, and fold into myself.

"We know you are trying," Crystal chimes in with her wishy-washy hippie voice. "You're not a bad girl, Melissa."

Her words send a rage through me. *What the ...? What the ...?* It's such garbage, trying to make it seem like everything's perfect just so they can feel perfect. My head feels like it will explode.

"Yes I am!" I snap. "Get it through your thick skulls. I *am* bad. A shitty person. Okay? I'm wicked ..." I try to think of the right word, but as usual the right word never comes. "... a wicked, wicked person." I push aside the coffee table and storm past. "Why are you pretending? Are you all fuckin' retards? I'm sick of this crap."

I slam the door to my room. My mother and her little posse of ladies can sit and plan my life all they want. I won't fucking do any of it. I just want them all to leave me alone. Let me live my life. Make my own mistakes. Stop trying to make me the good girl I'm not. Never will be. I turn on my music full blast and then fling my body down on the bed like I want to break it. Not the bed, my body.

Turn and run. Turn and run.

I hear the taunting words in my head again. The idea of leaving is so sweet. I could do it. I could leave right now, out my window. Live my own life. Make my own decisions. Drop out of school. Get a full-time job. I've met tons of people who've done it. And they're totally happy.

I look around my room. But what would I pack? How would I carry the stuff? I don't even have a bag. And what about my job? I couldn't just show up there on Monday, because the cops would be looking for me.

I stare at my cellphone and wish it would ring. Pray for it to ring. Order it to ring.

Eight days.

It's been eight days since I last saw him.

↜

Love messes you up. At first it's like being born again. You meet Life, real life, for the very first time and it gives you this heart full of love and happiness. And everything is as beautiful as it should be. But then suddenly it turns and walks away. And you stand there in shock, watching it go. You want to shout, "Wait a minute!" But it keeps walking. And you want to rip open your chest and throw your heart right back at it, wishing you'd never had a taste of love in the first place.

I get out my notebook and write another letter. The billionth one I have written to Michael.

The ink spills blue blood. I wish it were my blood. Bright, bright red, dead blood.

My heart is schizophrenic. One sentence is about how much I hate him. The next is about how much I love him. It goes on like that, back and forth, pacing. My pen is imprisoned on the paper. It can't get out. I know he'll think I'm crazy, but I can't stop myself. In the first few letters my words were good, like poetry. But now I write everything, anything. Threats. Lies. Warnings. In one letter, I say I'll kill myself. In another, I say I'm pregnant. And in another, I threaten I'll call the police and tell them about us. I write anything to get him to call. I don't care how crazy I sound, or pathetic or desperate. Because I *am* crazy and pathetic and desperate.

Ten

They say I have a few months to change my life. And if I don't ... what? I spend Christmas in juvenile detention? A diversion program? Screw that. They can't control my life, though I suppose they could put me in jail.

After school on Monday, I meet up with Jasmyn and Ally and tell them I'm thinking about running. They don't seem to be the slightest bit worried about their charges because their parents just don't care and they're not being forced to go to a different school. Jasmyn tells me to chill and says that chances are, since I'm white and innocent-looking and it's my first charge, they won't do anything anyway, so I don't need to panic. She's been charged three times and still hasn't gone to jail. "And I'm black!" she adds, like that's the proof right there. "The most they're gonna do is put you on house arrest, and that's a total joke, 'cause your ma ain't gonna call the cops on you. She'll just pretend she don't see what you do."

I know what Jasmyn says might be true, but to be honest, part of me kind of likes this ultimatum. 'Cause I want a new life. I want to *be* new.

As we walk to the park to smoke, Ally and Jasmyn start talking about the break-in night. They laugh hard about all of it, especially the fact I pissed my pants. I fall behind a little because I need to make a decision about my future, and my ADD doesn't let me talk and think at the same time. I haven't run yet, which sort of tells me I don't want to. I've done a lot of stupid things in my life, so if this was really what I wanted, I would have taken off that first night after the meeting at my house. So the fact I'm still around pretty much tells me I want this change. And sure, I want a new school and a new life, but the real reason I'd agree to go to the special school is because I want Michael back. And if changing my life does it, if being a good girl with a good future brings him back to me, I'll do it.

Eleven

Because I'm grounded, my mom and I split a bottle of white wine during dinner on Friday night. Though she has called and set up appointments for the new school, I still haven't agreed to go. I haven't talked to her all week and so I'm definitely not happy about staying home for the weekend. "If we're cooped up together, we may as well have a little fun," she says cheerily while pouring herself a full cup and giving me just half. She's trying to be nice and make things good between us, but I just can't help but be a bitch to her. I don't know why. There's no real reason. It's like it's instinctual with me.

"Hey..." I object, eyeing the half-empty glass. I am slouched back in the chair, arms crossed, making it clear that I'm not okay with the grounding, despite her attempt to make it fun.

She gives me a look. "That's enough for you, Hon," she says, but then she picks up the bottle and adds a little more. Which is pretty much how she is, always saying the right thing, like "You're grounded" or "No allowance," but in the end letting me get my own way. It's like she's a kid who is only acting the role of a parent. She can't possibly enforce a rule because she feels bad for me. It's as if she still feels all the pain of being young. Like instead of being thirty-five, she's only twenty.

She's decided to stay in tonight, which I know is a big deal to her. Usually she's out with one of her boyfriends, so I try to be good about it. I try to be happy, but my mind keeps wandering off.

We pop popcorn and make ice cream floats with Baileys. We get into our pyjamas and watch my mom's favourite movie: *Ice Castles*. It's this sappy movie from the '70s about a figure skater who goes blind and still wins the competition.

I look over to her near the end, already knowing how I'll find her. She's curled up in a ball, red-eyed and sniffling, using her sleeve to wipe her nose. If anyone walked in the room, they'd think she was my little sister. Already I've outgrown her. She's petite. And skinny. And beautiful, with darker olive skin and really nice blue eyes. Beside her I'm this clunky, beefy, pale girl with dark roots and the occasional pimple. Lucky me. I got all my father's genes — except for my boobs. My mom and I have great boobs.

I throw a cushion at her. "Jesus, Mom, stop crying, you've seen this a thousand times."

"I know. I know. I can't help it." She laughs at herself and then sniffles some more. I think the problem is that my mom has too much emotion, which makes us polar opposites. Sometimes I think that when she was pregnant with me, she sucked all the feelings out of me and kept them for herself.

I don't cry at movies, but I do sometimes lose it when I watch nature shows. Like the episode I saw last week about a leopard in a South African zoo. The leopard had just had a baby and the doctors were holding it because the baby was screaming in pain. And then one doctor discovered that the baby was missing a hind leg, and he put him back down because now he would not survive. He explained that the mother, in her excitement at delivering it, had severed the leg while chewing off the umbilical cord. The cub was so cute and so tiny, and his life was never even given a chance. Oh, I cried and cried and cried watching it alone on this cold metal surgery table. And I thought, how sad, because the mom would never understand the damage she caused.

⤆

Around eleven, I say I'm going to bed. In my room, I smoke a popper and stare at my cellphone. My mind is stuck on the thought of Michael.

Where did he go? Where did he go?

People don't just disappear like that. Leave without saying goodbye. Things so unfinished. It's like leaving in the middle of a sentence. I wish I didn't walk out that last night before he got to tell me why he wanted to break up. Then I'd at least know the reason instead of being left wondering what I did so wrong. Was it because of our age? Was it because of my suspension and that I don't do good in school? And to not say goodbye? Why? He loves me too much to say goodbye? Not enough? He's a coward? He had a breakdown? He had given hints about feeling low and there were signs I recognized from my mother's experiences with depression. Sweating. Staring vacantly at the television. Slow to respond to questions. Not being able to make simple decisions like what toppings to order on a pizza.

Or maybe he met another woman. I think of him in the arms of some lady, maybe someone his age, kissing her, holding her body when they sleep. This is what bothers me most—not so much the sex, but the sleeping. That warmth. That closeness. I think we have it all backward. Kids sleep alone and adults sleep together. It seems to me that kids are the ones who need the companionship, they are the ones who are haunted by the bogeyman. When I slept at Michael's, it was the first time I had been all night with someone while I was sober. And it was as if his sleeping body was a witness when the suffocating darkness violently woke me. And because of Michael, the night's grip on my throat was looser.

I just can't believe he left me.

If I stuffed my clothes in a garbage bag, if I just walked the fuck out of here, would I find him?

The phone rings, sending a wave of excitement through me, like it does every time since he left. "Hello?"

"Yo, Mel." The sound of a girl's voice sends my heart crashing back down. It's just Jessica. "We're in the ravine."

"Get yer ass over here, bee-yotch!" I hear Ally shouting into the phone.

"I'm grounded."

"So?" Jess questions, and then explains to Ally, "She's grounded."

"So?" Ally shouts.

"Okay. See you in twenty," I say, not needing any more persuasion than that.

"Later."

I hang up the phone and glare at it in my hand. "Fuck you." If Michael thinks I'm a child, I may as well act like one. I change into my jeans and a thick hoodie. I switch the phone onto vibrate and put it in my back pocket. Then I roll a blunt and slip out the window, hanging off the balcony, and drop from the second floor onto the first-floor balcony, then down.

⟳

The ravine party is totally sick by the time I'm there. It has to be past one o'clock. Everyone is scattered around the non-existent bonfire, sitting on the bench logs or on the grass. David has the tunes blasting, and there's so much ganja smoke in the air, you'd swear we're in the clouds. If people weren't so drunk, they might feel cold. But we party here all year, even in winter, so it seems our bodies just adapt to the temperature.

I find Jessica right away, sitting on her boyfriend Devon's lap. She passes me a mickey of vodka. "Here's to your grounding."

"Cheers," I say, taking the bottle and finishing what little was left.

"What the hell?" she contests.

"It's okay," Travis interjects before I can answer. "I've got some more." He takes a bottle out of a plastic bag by his feet and holds it up. Not caring what it is, I reach out and grab it, tearing off the cap and chugging down as much as I can before the burn in my throat becomes unbearable. The surrounding laughter overtakes Jessica's protest. I shut myself off from all of it, everyone, replace the cap on the bottle, throw it back to Travis and plop down onto the ground, staring up at the shadow of trees. There are many ways to run away, I think as my head spins. You can pack your bags and physically leave a place or you can stay and just pack up your soul.

At some point, Jessica, Travis, Devon, Ally, Craig, and I end up at Travis's house, in the basement, where we watch *Requiem for a Dream* again, for the fiftieth time.

A few hours later, I find myself lying half naked on Travis's parents' bed, trying to lose myself in the thought of Michael. All I'm thinking about is him. I'm imagining his mouth. I'm imagining his tongue. Craig is down between my legs, fully clothed. I won't touch him back. There's no way. He knows he could never go out with someone like me. I'm not the most beautiful, but guys like me. So he'll take what he can get—and all he can get is me off. I'm actually impressed at how good he is, and it takes only a few minutes. And when I'm done, I quickly push him away, pull up my underwear, and tell him I have to go.

"That's it?" he questions.

I turn my head, flipping my hair at the same time, and look him directly in the eyes. "What satisfaction canst thou have tonight?" I ask, quoting my favourite Claire Danes *Romeo and Juliet* line.

"Huh?"

Moron. I dismiss his ignorance. Of course he doesn't know Shakespeare. He's a little fifteen-year-old boy. "I'm grounded," I explain, zipping up my jeans. "It's like five in the morning. I have to get home."

He sits on the edge of the bed looking like some pathetic child, probably afraid to get up because of his hard-on. I don't feel sorry for him. He can go jerk off to some internet porn later. He'll get props for having been with me anyway. In the end, it will probably get him more action.

"Aren't you going to thank me?" I ask from the doorway, smirking. He looks at me out of the corner of his eye, shakes his head, and then pulls his gaze away. Usually I would finish with something even more obnoxious just to make him feel even shittier than he does right now. But instead, I'm the one who feels bad because I recognize in me the unfeeling and empty person I used to be, before meeting Michael. And I don't want her back.

"Good night," I say nicely, knowing it's too late to make a difference, and shut the door behind me.

Twelve

So I make a choice.

It's my first day at the Delcare Day Program. I stand outside the side entrance to the church, staring at the school door like it's an opponent I'm about to get in the ring with. I smoke a cigarette, pacing back and forth between the parking lot and the church, wondering what the fuck I'm doing. It's the hardest thing I've had to do. Go to a special school? It's like admitting you're a total failure. I feel sick to my stomach.

I suck in the last bit of cigarette wishing it would never end. It's the last in the pack. Finally, I butt it out.

Breathe.

I put my hand on the door.

Breathe.

Push.

The day program is in a church basement. There's something blasphemous about having a school for screwed-up teenagers in a church. It taints the holiness of the building or something. The sacred should be untouchable. It's like Metallica playing a concert in the Roman Coliseum, or relocating our crappy school band practice to the library due to flooding. I feel like me being here puts an embarrassing brown streak on God's clean white underwear.

I head down the stairs to the classroom. I saw it yesterday at my intake meeting. There are a bunch of little elementary school desks scattered in uneven rows, a few larger round tables, and a teacher's desk in the corner. Along one wall are painted blue and yellow "cubbyholes" where we can leave our jackets and stuff. On the other walls are old laminated posters of Michael Jordan, Martin Luther King, and people climbing mountains. Across the hall is "the couch room," which is a windowless room full of mismatched, worn couches and a big square table in the centre full of pamphlets on STDs, drugs, Kids Help Line.

The teacher, Miss Something, a middle-aged woman with the kind of hippie beaded necklace my mom's friend Crystal would wear, meets me outside the classroom and reviews our conversation from yesterday's meeting. "Now remember, Melissa, you're here to work on what's keeping you from being successful in the regular school system. It's a transition program. We are committed to help you work on your personal challenges. Okay?"

"Okay," Echo answers.

"The program is for the hardest-to-serve, highest-risk students in the school board. I tell you that because some students think they're here just like regular school, and they're surprised when we challenge them. We need to make sure you're ready to work hard with us in making some long-term changes. We want to inspire you to change, Melissa. Are you ready?" she asks, with a big smile, like I'm about to be shown the prize behind curtain number three.

"Ready," Echo answers.

Miss puts her arm on my shoulder and escorts me into the room. She shows me to my seat. It's about ten o'clock, so the other students are already there, working. I sit down at a desk at the back, but it's so small I can barely squeeze my legs underneath. Talk about regression back to childhood. I think it's intentional, the desks, the cubbyholes. I think they want you to recall your pure kid self, a time before you got ruined.

Miss puts a sheet of paper on my desk and tells me I have one hour to complete the orientation exercise. "Do you have a pen?" she asks me.

"No," I lie, because I don't want to look like a keener.

"She can have my pen," a skinny guy two desks away says, and flings the pen at me so I have to duck to avoid it.

"Tyler!" Miss shouts.

"What?" The pimple-faced shit smirks, and his hands go up in the air. "Just offering."

"You don't throw things across the classroom. And you know full well what you're doing." She turns to me. "I apologize, Melissa." I'm amazed she doesn't even look upset. She calmly gives me her pen and heads toward the guy's desk, leans down, taps her finger on the desktop, and says, "I'll see you in the couch room, now." And then she keeps walking.

"Why? What did I do?" Tyler protests, but she just keeps walking, her back to him, like she's heard it a million times. "What, trying to help and what ... what?" Tyler keeps mumbling as he gets up and walks out. On his way, he looks back at me and gives me the finger.

"Fuck you," I say loudly back, because no little shit like him is going to dick me around. Everyone looks at me now, including Miss.

"Tyler. Go. Now," Miss says firmly, and points to the door. She gives me a teacherish I'll-deal-with-you-later disapproval glance and walks out, leaving Sheila the CYC (child and youth counsellor) sitting in the corner in charge.

Unaffected, I start the test. It asks me questions about my past school, about my attitude with teachers, and about my future goals. I take the time to casually glance around the room at the other four students, three guys and one girl. Despite what happened, no one is staring at me or even glancing my way. Not 'cause they're scared; with the exception of Tyler, they all look like they can hold their own. It's more like they couldn't care less if I exist or not. Which is all very fine with me. I don't talk to anyone that day. Tyler is sent home. Miss tells me that I didn't really get off to a good start, but she again apologizes about Tyler's behaviour. At the same time, she says if I use "foul language" in class, I too will be sent home in the future.

Strangely enough, I actually like the school, 'cause I can concentrate, and it's clear everyone is dealing with their own crap and no one is here to make friends. And that's exactly fine with me. In fact it's perfect, 'cause it gives me the hope that finally I might be able to learn something. And maybe it's possible that I will be a veterinarian and get the life I want.

Thirteen

I knew it would be a big deal when Craig let out word that he hooked up with me. The guys at my regular school usually like me, so since I've been with Michael they've wondered why I stopped screwing around with them. They would never have guessed it was because I had a boyfriend. They would just joke and say I turned dyke. But now that the word is out I messed around with Craig, Jess tells me that there are at least five guys asking about me. Which is kind of nice. I guess you could say I have status, because before Michael I'd do whatever—sex, blow job, whatever. I'm good at it. At the same time, guys can't mess me up because I'm cool with everything. I do it 'cause I like it, and so I'm not one of these girls that goes around crying because she thought it meant more than it did. Or the ones who get jealous and possessive, thinking that just because they hook up in the washroom with a guy, it means they're going out. Those girls end up looking like idiots. They don't realize that if it doesn't mean anything to you, then no one can hurt you. That way, you're in control.

But Ally, she's different than me. Her situation is that she'll mess around with guys only to get stuff. If you hear she was with someone, or texted them some raunchy photos of herself, it's because she's after something. Like a school assignment. Or weed. Or money. Or once, one guy's sister's leather jacket.

Jess doesn't mess around with anyone, because she likes having a boyfriend. But she's no angel. She'll set it up for Ally or some other girls. Her brother is one year older, so his friends will come to her when they're horny. She's like a pimp. And she likes all the drama that the hookups create. It gives her power. She's like peacekeeper and provoker all in one.

⟶

Sometimes my counsellor, Eric, likes to make me feel bad about being with so many guys. He's just too old to understand what happens now. I tell him I don't do it because of "peer pressure," I do it for me. "An orgasm is better than any drug," I say. When you think about it, people get high to escape, to forget things, to release stress, and to leave their entire mortal existence. So how is that different than an orgasm? In a way the most natural, always available, free high is inside your body.

Ms. Switzer says poets used to call an orgasm "death" because it's one of the only times you can leave your body and consciousness for a few seconds without being dead. "There's wisdom in that," I tell Eric.

I tell Eric about only some of the guys I had sex with before Michael, maybe half. He says it's okay that some people like to have sex more than others. And after covering all the safety things, like STDs and rape and stuff, he changes his story and says he's really concerned and wants to be sure I'm doing it for the right reasons.

"I'm sorry, it's weird to say this," I confess flippantly, "but I just like to cum." I quickly look to see how he'll respond. I stare straight at him because I know it makes him uncomfortable and sometimes I just like shocking people.

Eric sticks out his lower lip and nods his head, like he's impressed with my answer. Then he opens his hands from their prayer-like position in a sort of gesture of acceptance. "Women have certainly come a long way. There was a time not too long ago that a girl would never admit that. In fact, she'd probably never even experience an orgasm until she was older. It's great to have confidence in your sexual needs."

"You people make such a big deal about sex. Especially girls doing it. When guys play around, it's no big deal. I bet you have guys in here that screw around and you don't say anything to them."

"Sure I do. I call them on it right away. I try to encourage them to take the girls' feelings into consideration."

"Some guys get mad at me. You know, for not doing anything back? Like last weekend I was with this Craig, who's sort of geeky. He went down on me because, you know, that's as much as he could ever get from a girl like me. I mean, sometimes they're just lucky to get anything. So he went down, and then after that he was like, 'Okay, now my turn,' and he started to undo his fly, and I was like, 'No way!'"

Eric was so engrossed in my story that he forgot his therapist-self and laughed in amazement. "So he basically serviced you?"

"So? That's what guys usually do, isn't it? Anyway, it pissed me off. Like *really* pissed me off. He made such a big deal of it. He got so mad, he started spreading rumours at school about me being a slut and a whore."

"Of course, the name calling is totally unjustified. But I'm kind of surprised you got so angry at him. That you wouldn't think that this sexual act you're both engaging in would lead him to conclude he was going to get some pleasure in return.

Did you know it's actually painful for men to be aroused for long periods of time without release?"

"Blue balls. So?"

He pauses. Swallows. Licks his lips. Recrosses his legs. "I just don't want you to be in a dangerous situation. Some men can get quite aggressive if their needs aren't met. You really need to be careful."

"It wasn't dangerous. What are you saying? Return the favour even if I don't want to?"

"No," he says firmly. Clears his throat again. "No. Of course not."

"So I don't get it, then. What are you saying?"

Eric moves again in his chair. It squeaks. Suddenly things become awkward. "I guess I'd like you to take into consideration your partner's needs. Healthy sex is often about two people, mutual pleasure. It's not a singular act, or else it would be masturbation."

"Okay. So what do the guys do when you tell them that? Do you think they listen to what you say and start to get their girls off?"

"I can't change anyone's behaviour, Melissa."

"You know what I think? When you say it to the guys, I think it goes in one ear and out the other. And you probably don't lose any sleep over it."

"Let me ask you something. How do you feel when it's over? When you go home and you're falling asleep in bed? Do you feel sad? Empty? Happy? Lonely? Exhilarated?"

"Powerful," I say, without even having to think about it too much.

Eric opens his mouth, ready to pounce on my answer, but before he can say anything else, I look up at the clock. It's ten past five. "Ding! Session's up. Gotta go," I announce, and get up from my chair.

Fourteen

The place where I was most happy with Michael was in bed, even though we didn't have sex.

When the world was shut out and it was just me and Michael and his sheets and his closed blinds, I was in heaven. We'd lie in the dark watching TV or a DVD, and then he'd make me watch the news. Truthfully, I didn't care what I watched as long as I was lying on his chest, feeling his heart beating under my ear.

And usually, at some point, we started making out, like we were twelve years old or something. We never even got totally naked. It usually started with me teasing a hand up his leg, farther and farther, closer and closer, until I could see a bulge shaping through his jeans. Till I heard his breath, and my head moved with the pounding of his heart. Till I knew he couldn't stand it any longer.

After that, sometimes we'd order a pizza. Or sometimes we'd play Scrabble, and I'd joke how it made me feel a million years old, until I started to kick his ass at it. Sometimes we'd be silly. I'd play tic-tac-toe with a pen on his stomach. Or he'd try to balance a pepperoni slice on my nose. But most of the time we just talked about stuff like our childhoods and friends and parents. And about heavy shit. Like him having to deal with his mother, who has an eating disorder and was hospitalized. Or his depression, which forced him to drop out of university. Or about my father, who left my mom when I was small, and how I wasn't interested in finding him because I knew it would only be a disappointment.

"Are you sure?" he asked.

I searched my head, thinking about his question. "Yeah. I know that's not an exciting answer. But it's like, 'Fuck you.' You know? What am I going to do, ruin my life because he's a loser?"

"Sometimes I'm amazed you're only sixteen."

"Just turned …" I reminded him.

"Well, anyway. You've lived a lot of life already."

"How come you're the only one who thinks that I'm amazing?"

His answer was to pull me closer. Which was the perfect response, because sometimes words aren't the best way to answer a question.

And I'd wished I could stay there forever. On that bed. In those sheets. In that summer. I wished that I could just lie there in my underwear and play silly games and bare my honest soul to someone. But eventually and always, I had to get dressed. And with each piece of clothing, I felt myself disappear under the layers.

Socks / daughter.

Shirt / whore.

Jeans / student.

Hoodie / friend.

Studded belt / bitch.

Fifteen

Michael made me a different person. He made me want to be a better person. Sometimes I'm embarrassed at how stupid I was with him. I used to make him greeting cards out of construction paper and glue on ribbons. And I cried in front of him all the time. About nothing. It was like I was my mother. I'd just come through the door and fall into the cushy couch and bawl while he'd get me some juice and whatever food he had around. Then he'd sit beside me, pull me close to him, and just rub the back of my head. And when I finally stopped my blubbering and was calm enough to tell him what was wrong, I couldn't think of anything to say because my words would have sounded so dumb by that point: Ally was being a bitch, I failed a science exam, my mom got drunk last night. Big deal.

Usually I'd start to tell him all this but then, in the middle of it, I'd just start laughing at my own pathetic self, and he'd start laughing and then we'd kiss, and my mouth would be on his, sucking in his happiness like he was some kind of helium making me light again.

Even my voice would get all squeaky and high-pitched, and I'd giggle like a little girl.

"I just don't get how he could leave me," I tell Jess over the phone after going over it for the millionth time.

"Don't be a stupid idiot," she comforts me. "You are twelve years younger than him. He couldn't take it, Melissa. The fact that he left you proves he loved you. It was too much for him. If he didn't love you, he would have stuck around and just duped you. You see? He had to leave. Put a barrier between your love. It's so romantic, really."

"Yeah, tragic."

"Yeah. Tragic. Anyway, he'll probably come back," Jess speculates. "He's probably just confused. You guys were really in love."

I want to believe what she says, because of all my friends, Jess knows the most about love. She has a good boyfriend. She and Devon have been together for eight months and they've never had a fight. But that's because he's so dull he could never bring his heart rate up high enough to get upset about anything.

I call Ally next. Big mistake.

"You need to forget about him," she blurts out, and then puts me on hold to answer the other line. She was always jealous of Michael and me. I know she's tired of me talking about him all the time. Even I am getting sick of me. "He's a loser. It's his loss," she adds when she comes back.

"You can't stop loving someone just like that, you know. You can't just turn it off."

"Well, he did."

"Shut up."

"Well, he did."

"He was good to me," I persist.

I can hear Ally's eyes rolling. "Whatever."

I make up a reason to get off the phone. I don't need to hear that. I know he loved me. What we had here was real. And even if it wasn't, I'm still grateful for it all, because my heart isn't dead like before. Sure, it's a pathetic, wheezing, oozing open wound, but it's not dead. And I'd rather it be whimpering than numb.

Sixteen

I come home after the day program and my mother's bedroom door is closed. I see our superindendent Giovanni's grimy shoes in the front hall, and his dumb-ass waist pouch on the couch.

I grab a Coke and chips and go back out. I don't want to be in there when they're together. I don't want to see Giovanni come out of the room, his hairy fat belly hanging over his ugly tighty-whiteys, shuffling off to the bathroom.

Giovanni and my mother have been screwing for years, almost ever since we moved in. I don't know what to make of it. I used to not have a clue, but now that I'm older, they don't hide it. It's like he's the man *around* the house without being the man *in* the house. He fixes our toilet. He bleeds our rads each fall. He hooked up our cable TV to the new satellite dish. And when my mom's car got smashed up in the parking lot, Giovanni had the guy in a headlock until he coughed up his ID and insurance papers.

"He's a nice person," my mom explained one night. "We have a good time together. But it is what it is. It'll never be more, and we're both happy with that. There are some men who just can't be in a relationship."

"So why are you with him?"

She pauses, fluttering her long, overly mascaraed eye-lashes, which means she's thinking hard about this one. "Because it's easy, I suppose." She takes a long, pensive drag on her cigarette.

What I don't ask is if she tells her boyfriends about him. Or if she's getting a reduction in rent. Or if she's fucking him because she's using him. But I don't think it's as clear as that. I don't think they even spend much time worrying about it. It's just this unspoken thing that happens. And I suppose that's what sex is sometimes.

"Sometimes sex is just sex," my mom said one time. "Sometimes it's love. Sometimes it's a physical need. Sometimes it's a barter."

"Barter?"

"You know. Like a currency. That happens even in marriages. You know, the wife wants a new kitchen, so she puts out. It's sort of weird."

"Weird," Echo repeats, pretending not to know what she's talking about. But truthfully, I get it.

It's like me having sex with Sid, the boy in my building whom I've known for a thousand years. He likes me. He always has. So every once in a while, before I met Michael, we'd screw around. Why? Because there's some kind of obligation, some kind of guilt, I suppose. He's always giving me alcohol or weed, whenever I want it, so it's sort of just understood. I try to find other sources, but it's hard to give up something that's free. I suppose, if I were honest, I'd say I sleep with him because of all this. But it doesn't feel that way when we're together. It doesn't feel icky, though most of the time I'm high. It just feels, well … like sex. A climax. A shudder. An absence from my life. And then a beautiful, beautiful stillness.

It's ironic that the one person I love, the greatest love of my life, won't have sex with me. Michael said it wasn't right. That we'd wait until I was eighteen, when he'd marry me. But we did mostly everything else, which was confusing at first, because I didn't see a difference. But the longer we went without having sex, the more I realized just how amazing sex was. How much I longed for him to be inside me. Not in a sex way, but in a love way.

Now I know there's nothing more beautiful than sex between two people who are truly in love. That's real sex. And the longer you wait, the more sure you are, the act becomes something so much bigger than any physical sensation. And I think even if Michael had changed his mind, even if he wanted to, I'd have said to wait until we were married. I think I loved him that much.

With Michael, I didn't see love happening. It's like one day, out of the blue, he kissed me, or rather we kissed each other. I don't think it was premeditated in any way. It simply happened. At work, by the sterilizing machine. When we were both bending down to check if the surgical utensils were ready.

"Wow," I reflected like an idiot after it happened.

"Yeah. Wow." Was he making fun of me?

"What was that?" I asked, still bewildered.

"I think it was a kiss." Now *he* sounded like the idiot.

Then we did it again. More. I pushed my face onto his, opened my mouth. My whole body was on fire. I fell in love, right then. It felt so right.

"How did you learn to kiss like that?" he said, pulling away and simultaneously wiping his mouth.

"Do I kiss by the book?"

"What?"

"Am I good?" I paraphrase, smiling proudly.

"Too good for eighteen."

"I'm sixteen."

"Shut up," he said, putting his finger over my lips.

I opened my mouth and took his whole finger inside, sucking.

"Ughh!" He pulled away his finger and made a face like I was the Devil.

I'd done something wrong. "Sorry." I was embarrassed. Was it childish? Normally a guy would have liked it. They always do.

"It's okay." He opened the door of the sterilizer and pulled out the tray. The room instantly smelled sanitized.

"I'm not a virgin, you know," I said, following him down the hall to the operating table, where poor Dexter the daschund was spread-legged on his back, ready to be snipped.

He laughed, stopped, and looked at me. "It was just a kiss."

"I know."

⟵

But it wasn't just a kiss. We avoided each other for the entire next week, but I couldn't stop thinking about him. It wasn't like I was thinking about his body or kissing or anything like that. I went over every conversation we'd ever had. I imagined living with him. Making him dinner. I imagined marrying him. Having his children. Growing old together. Dying together, and then being buried side by side in the same cemetery. It was going to be perfect. Like it all made sense now, as if everything in my life had been leading up to us getting together.

⟵

The next time we kissed was when he gave me a lift home in his hatchback Volkswagen that stinks 'cause its diesel. We talked the whole way about music and work.

Finally we pulled up to my apartment building. "It's ugly," I remarked apologetically.

"It's just a building," he said. "Everybody has the same four walls. It's what's inside that matters."

"Yeah. Well. The inside is pretty much the same. Thanks for the lift," I said, pulling my knapsack onto my lap. I looked directly at him, waiting for him to kiss me.

"You're welcome." His hands remained fixed on the steering wheel.

"Aren't you going to kiss me?"

He laughed. "I wasn't thinking about it."

"Liar."

I waited, but he didn't move, so I leaned over and kissed him. He kissed back. And we kissed for a long time. The sloppy wet sounds were unavoidably awkward until he reached out and turned up the radio. We kissed some more. Then he stopped, like he was suddenly aware of something, and started to look around outside the car.

I pulled back. "What happened?"

"Nothing." He sat up and put his hands back on the wheel. "I better go."

"Okay," I said in my "whatever" tone, pissed off that he couldn't face up to what he was really thinking. What—I'm too young? I'm poor? Ugly? Dumb? Slutty? "See ya when I see ya," I said, and slammed the door shut before hearing his response.

The passenger-side window went down. "Melissa!"

"What?" I poked my head into the car.

"We could meet for coffee sometime. Or a movie?"

"Movie's good." I smiled. "Give me a call," I said coolly, but my heart was racing.

Seventeen

I decide to cut my appointment with Eric today. I've gone to school every day, every period, this week, and I'm tired and I feel too busy to make the effort.

I've been seeing Eric for almost two years, ever since I started skipping school more, getting into fights, and doing more than just pot. My social worker, who until lately only talked to me once a year, hooked me up. She used to do more when I was about twelve, for a couple years after my little brother Bradley died, and then it was only a phone call or visit every once in a while until I got my charge.

Eric's office is on the main floor of a creaky old house that is now a family services agency. He's an okay guy. I'm sure there are better counsellors out there. He's nice enough. Honest. He's got a good sense of humour and he's sort of simple. Not "simple" as in stupid, but simple as in "easy." Anyway, he's definitely better than the last counsellor I saw for only two sessions when I was twelve, after Bradley died. All I did with her was draw pictures and play with dolls, which was pretty much a waste of time.

I don't know what I'm actually getting out of the whole thing. It's not like I've got some major trauma that can explain me. Sometimes people are just not explainable. Even if your parents are great and you have a nice house, you can still be messed up.

It's annoying that people like Eric or my teachers keep asking me why I'm making the choices I make. I have no answer for them. I just do. I don't sit around and think about why. It just happens. I think it's just that some people are born a bad crop. Born wicked. And there's not much anyone can do to steer you off the path you're destined for. Wait—I take that back. Maybe they could nudge you a little from side to side to keep you steady, but generally, I think people are driven by something mysterious inside.

My mom tells me to consider going to Eric like going to a job, that I'm making an investment in myself which will pay off later. Jasmyn tells me to think of it as a stay-out-of-jail card. "Judges like that counselling shit," she advises.

Usually, Eric and I don't talk about anything really big. It's not like in the movies, where you see people lying on a couch and confessing life traumas. It's normally just about my week or what's happening with friends or guys. Sometimes we talk about my mom. Once we talked about my father and why I don't give a shit about his existence. Most of the time, if we talk about anything real important, it's about my little brother Bradley. I suppose that's my trauma, if I had to pick one.

⌐

Bradley was only six when he died of leukemia. We had spent two years going back and forth to the hospital, and for a while it looked like he was going to be okay. I remember doing arts and crafts, watching videos, and playing Sorry on his hospital bed. A few times he came home, and things would be fine. But then, just before Christmas, he got really sick. We took him back into the hospital and he never came back out.

Over the two years, my mother spent a lot of nights there with him, sleeping on a squeaky plastic-coated bench in the room. Crystal would stay with me at home. I'd be so jealous he got to spend time with Mom alone. Sometimes, on weekends, I got to sleep in the room too, but the nurses had to keep it quiet because only one person was allowed to stay over. I'd sneak into his bed and curl up next to him, and when the nurses came in to check his vitals, they'd just give this adoring look at the two of us.

Before he got sick, Bradley was a pain-in-the-ass little brat, but as soon as he went into the hospital, he became pale and cute, and I felt bad for being so mean to him all the time. As time goes on, the cuter he becomes in my memory, and the guiltier I feel about giving him such a hard time.

The thing with Bradley was that when he was around, we were a family. It wasn't just him being an innocent little kid that made our home happy. It was that we were all linked, connected in some way. Grounded, I guess. It didn't seem to matter we didn't have a father around. We felt complete. My mom was happy almost all the time, so she didn't miss work or get fired. And I guess I was happy too. I can't entirely remember, but it's like I think of myself then and I can see my face in the memories; I can see my smile. And I don't know what the hell I was so happy about, except that there was nothing yet to be miserable about. I think that's just growing up — you grow into misery and complication.

My mother and I don't talk about what happened next. After Bradley died, she got depressed and began drinking and was a real mess. She couldn't work. She couldn't do anything.

We lost our apartment, and we had to live at a shelter for a few months until Crystal got us an apartment in her building and helped my mom get back on track. Except my mom never really went back to "normal," the way she was before. And I don't think I ever felt we were a family after that.

So it's no wonder it's a time my mom and I just want to forget about. But it's not like we ever forget Bradley. There are photographs of him all over the apartment. Other than doing something special on his birthday, though, we rarely mention his name. We don't need to. He's always there. He's always here.

So instead of going to see Eric, I meet up with Ally to blaze in the alley behind her house. We sit inside an old wood garage where she and people in her neighbourhood go to chill when it's cold out. It's got some plastic jugs to sit on, and a little table made of plywood propped up on milk crates. Usually someone's in there, smoking or drinking or just chilling, but this time we're alone. Ally just got her nose pierced and wanted me to see it. It doesn't look good. Her nose is sort of pug-like and you need a nice pointy nose for a piercing to look good. She says she's trying to look more girlie because she thinks she looks too much like a guy. Truth is, I think she's gay but she just doesn't want to admit it yet.

"It's 'cause your hair is so short," I say, which it is. It's like a boy's—plain and brown and short. "Grow it. And stop wearing those butch guy jeans," I suggest.

"Yeah," she agrees, but she won't do it.

We stay there for about an hour, while she tells me what's happening with everyone at school. While she talks, I compose a letter to Michael in my head.

Michael,

Sometimes you occupy everything in my sight and in my mind. No matter what I do, all I think about is you, all I see is you. You're this heavy, solid mass standing directly in front of me, like a door, and beyond you life is happening. I try to look beyond. I try to strain my neck to peek around, or stand on my tippytoes, or slip underneath. But it's hopeless. You block everything I experience, everything but the edges.

"It was hilarious in class today. You know Aiden, right? He's friends with Mark? He's always causing shit, but in a funny way, you know? And so …"

Other times, you're not so solid. During those times it's like I'm living two lives at once, and I can easily pull myself in and out of them. It's like looking out a subway window when you're stuck in the tunnel. I can see what's on the subway behind me, but I can also see through the window. It's like I'm simultaneously looking backward and forward. It's like that with you. All I have to do is slightly change my focus and you're there.

"… then the whole class went silent, and I was like, 'Shit' …"

No matter what, you're there. Every thought is brought back to you. While waiting for the bus. While sitting in class. While watching TV. While doing my homework. While sitting here, in the alley, talking to Allison.

"… Mr. Burns walked up to the desk and held his hand out. Aiden was so busted. *So* busted. And he pretended there was nothing in his lap. I think he was trying to get rid of the Baggie …"

How was your day? What did you eat? Do you feel better? Who did you talk to? Do you miss home? Do you miss me? Do you think of me?

"… and he just jumped up and knocked over the desk and went out the fucking window! … Melissa? Melissa?" Ally jabs me in the arm.

"Hah!" I respond, pretending I'm laughing at her bullshit story.

"Fuck." She abruptly blows her smoke out. "It's like talking to a fucking corpse."

"Sorry. I *was* listening … He took off out the window and …?"

"Don't pull that Echo shit with me," she says.

"I'm not. It's not that." I try to bring myself back into this miserable, boring world, but I just can't fake it. I just can't fake I care. I know she's angry about me going to another school, but I've got other problems to worry about. "Sorry. Fuck. My head hurts."

"Well, your head hurts a lot lately. You probably have a fucking brain tumour."

"Thanks."

"No problem."

"Listen, I'm gonna split," I say, butting out my smoke and picking up my bag. I walk away, knowing she's staring at my back. Probably hurt or some shit, but I can't really be bothered to care. Then, on my way home, I start to feel bad about it. I should have made her feel better. I should have at least pretended to be interested.

Eighteen

In a way, Bradley was lucky to stay a kid forever, immortalized in perfect *kid-ness*. The world is much easier to understand when you're young, because everything is black and white: good and bad, nice and mean, beautiful and ugly. You learn this in fairy tales. And it's comforting to know exactly which category everyone falls into.

But then you get older and it's like the black and white merge into this murky grey. There's confusion and anger because no one fits perfectly anymore. You start to see people as whole beings, lovable and hateable at the same time. And this messiness comes along with a whole new frustration. The stepmother who was a bitch suddenly seems sort of smart. Mr. Howard, the nice grade-four teacher, is starting to look like a bit of a pervert in the school photo. And the mother you blindly defended for so long suddenly starts to seem a little irresponsible.

And that's a hell of a lot to deal with, when all you want to do is come home, eat chips, and watch TV.

Take for example my uncle Freestyle (whose real name is Brian). Growing up, I could see he was clearly an asshole — an irresponsible, obnoxious drunk, a bad father, and a cruel man who would come to our apartment every week or so to terrorize my mother. I used to slam the door in his face and throw the TV converter at his head. All I knew was what my mother told me — "He's a deadbeat loser" — and all I saw was my mother in a crying, pathetic heap when he left.

But then Uncle Freestyle became sort of good. When I was about thirteen, he started to talk to me out on the balcony. We'd share a spliff and he'd ask me about guys and school and Mom. And he actually listened. It felt as if he cared. And he didn't judge me, like I was a kid. He just seemed to get it. So we started doing this more and more, smoking weed together. And then he'd give me a big bag of it, for free at first, and I started to sell it to my friends. Not like a real dealer, but I make a bit of extra cash. It's all sort of unspoken, but I think he feels good for helping me out. I've been saving the money for university. He said I'd never get there with my mom being such a financial wreck.

"If you want to walk on water, you need to get out of the boat, Melissa," he'd say. Which basically means if you want success in life, you first have to take risks.

Uncle Freestyle always says these little bits of wisdom. I write them down in my journal, and sometimes I draw them out in coloured bubble letters and tape them on the wall around my bed. That saying is my favourite. I stare at it while lying in bed trying to fall asleep, which sometimes takes hours. *Get out of the boat, Melissa. Get out of the boat.* I know the saying actually has something to do with Jesus, but when I'm drifting off to sleep I imagine myself lying down in this Lady of Shalott wooden rowboat. I imagine I'm wearing a puffy white dress, with those lace-trimmed long-underwear pantaloons underneath. My hair is long and is tied back with purple satin ribbons. Above me is blue sky. I stretch a foot out over the edge of the bed and imagine it dangling over the water. The boat rocks. There's hesitation. I look over the edge. Black depths. A deep breath. And I think to myself, *Get out of the boat. Get out of the boat.*

That's my other favourite saying. Well, it's not a saying at all, it's a poem. I don't know exactly what "The Lady of Shalott" is supposed to be about. We read it in English class. Ms. Switzer said a poem can mean anything you want it to mean, as long as it makes sense to you.

Basically, the Lady of Shalott is a woman who has some kind of spell cast upon her that dooms her to the task of weaving all day. She lives in a tower on this tiny island and is separated from the rest of life by a river. On the other side of the river is a road that leads to Camelot, where all the rich and free people get to go and enjoy their lives. For some reason, the curse prevents her from looking directly outside, so she must use a mirror to reflect the happenings on the road. That's how detached from life she is. She watches wedding and funeral processions pass by and she's sad about it because she can't join them, but she goes on with her weaving because that's what her life is. But then one day she sees two newlyweds making out on the riverbank and she feels terribly lonely. A while later Prince Lancelot comes along and skinny-dips his hot bod in the river right in front of her tower. She's so amazed by him, she takes her eyes off the mirror and looks directly at him. She instantly falls in love, but she's miserable because she knows she will never have him, or that life. So she stops weaving. She finds a boat. Writes her name on it. Gets in the boat and dies of a broken heart, leaving her body to drift into Camelot.

I know that's only my interpretation. I know there's stuff about the river cracking and reflections and historical things, but this is what it is to me.

The most tragic part comes at the end, when a crowd gathers around this woman lying dead in the boat, and Lancelot makes his way through the crowd and says, "She has a lovely face. God in his mercy lent her grace." And it's like, given another life, he would have fallen in love with her. Given another life, they could have been together.

Oh God ... my heart melts at that point. And when I really think about it, when I read the poem, I can't help but feel really sad. I completely understand how she feels, watching life and people pass by on a road she will never join. I saw it when Crystal took me to a fancy sports club for lunch one time. Or at McDonald's on a Sunday night, when nice little families pack the tables. The life I can never reach is all around me. But to fall in love with someone on that road? That's the tragedy. To fall in love with someone you can never have. Is there any greater pain? The Lady could bear anything else — loneliness, boredom, isolation. But unrequited love? Any other loss wouldn't be worth dying for.

Nineteen

The thing about these special school day programs is that they stick a bunch of messed-up teenagers together and think somehow this will help us get better. Imagine a room full of druggy, angry teenagers. We just all feed off each other's stresses, and the only good that comes of it is that some of us end up thanking God we're not as bad as the next guy. They should make a school where there's a mix of good kids, like reclusive scholar students, and bad druggy kids, so that we could all rub off on each other.

It's an intense Thursday morning. Keenan, a seventeen-year-old guy who just got out of a residential drug program, storms into the couch room, pissed off and making sure everyone knows it. We are all sitting around discussing current events, which we do every morning. After each of us reads a part of the newspaper, Sheila, the CYC, asks us to share our thoughts.

When Keenan walks in, a girl named Snow is talking about some convenience store owner who was stabbed in the neck but survived. And how the next day he won two hundred thousand dollars in the lottery. Keenan, obviously demanding that everyone in the room be brought down to his miserable level, sits slouched on the chair, legs wide apart, baggy jeans drooping, baseball cap over his face, and yawns loudly.

"Thanks, Snow," Sheila says, then she turns her head. "Keenan, can you sit up please?"

Keenan doesn't move.

"Keenan? We need you up. And I need to see your eyes."

The room gets tense. I don't know how air, something that's invisible, can all of a sudden grow heavy and thick with stress, but it does. And we all know this is not going to end well. Keenan is crazy. He comes to school half doped up on medication just to calm him down. Apparently his father, a motorcycle gang member, shot his mother in the gut and Keenan watched her bleed to death when he was a kid. So, really, no one can blame him for being a little nuts.

Fearless Sheila gets up and moves in toward him. "Keenan?"

He startles, pretending she's woken him up. "What?" he snaps, incredibly annoyed at her interference.

"Let's go," Sheila says calmly, motioning out toward the hallway. "Let's talk about it in the classroom."

He turns his head and looks off to the side, ignoring her.

"Come on, man, give her a break," Tyler pipes up, and it's all Keenan needs. He's up out of his chair in two seconds, towering over scrawny Tyler, who only has time to throws his knees up to defend himself against Keenan's arms reaching in and lifting him up like a curled ball off the chair.

"Keenan!" Sheila shouts, but the two intertwined bodies are already on the floor. Jordie, this real big fat guy who's been in the program only two days, steps in between them and they part too easily, as if they had been waiting for someone to cut in.

Sheila, all red-faced now, takes Keenan by the elbow and leads him outside. Jordie holds on to Tyler by the back of his hoodie and then pushes him down into the couch. The rest of us—Snow, this girl Kat, and me—just sit there, staring at each other. Tyler has a bloody lip, which makes his pimply, ugly face even uglier. I actually feel sorry for him since I've come to realize he's pretty harmless.

"That was brave," Snow says to him. "Stupid, but brave. You know he's fucked up?"

"Yeah," Tyler admits, and puts his hand to his lip. "It wasn't brave. I just do shit without thinking. Sometimes it's good shit. Sometimes it's bad."

"There's a bong in the girls' washroom," I offer as condolence. Since I've got to know him, I think he's sort of sweet. He's been through so much—foster homes since he was five, and now a group home where he has to basically fight older and bigger guys for everything. It's like he's a harmless little runt fighting for the teat. "Look in the garbage bin, under the plastic."

"Thanks," he says, and gets up, probably not to go smoke it but just to get the hell out of the room.

The teacher (whom I no longer call just Miss), Ms. Dally, appears at the door before he gets to it. Obviously Sheila is dealing with Keenan and has given her the lowdown, and she's come to pull things together. "Where are you going?" she demands.

"Wash my lip," Tyler says quickly.

She inspects his face. "Okay. When you're done, go into my office." She turns to the rest of us and smiles. Ms. Dally has this way of being totally calm even after students dump on her or spaz out or just plain give her attitude. It's not like she doesn't have feelings, it's more like she's seen it all and nothing stresses her anymore. "Well, ladies and gentlemen ... not even 9:15 and it's been quite the morning already. Let's go to class!"

And that's that. Tyler doesn't return for three days, we never see Keenan again, and nobody asks where he's gone.

Twenty

Everyone is really on me about these three months before the court date, and it seems like even though I'm trying to be good—going to school, meeting my curfew most of the time, not doing so many drugs—no one tells me I'm doing better. My probation officer calls the day program to check how I'm doing. Then the social worker calls the probation officer and sometimes my mother. And then the day program calls my mother. And my mother calls Eric. That's how it goes, so, really, I don't have to tell anyone anything. They all already know, even though they pretend not to. Sometimes it pisses me off. It feels as if there are too many adults sticking their noses into my business, and I just want to be left alone.

Since I skipped my last session with Eric, I have to go see him this week, but that doesn't mean I have to actually "be there." An hour can go by quickly, and even when it's filled with talking, it's possible to leave without having said anything. I especially don't feel like going into any details, so today I am Echo with Eric. I just let him ask the questions.

"How's school?"

"How's school?" Echo repeats. "It's easy. There are only six kids. But that changes all the time. It's chilled, so no one is in your business and you just do your work. And if you're upset about something, you can take a break or go out for a smoke. Teacher's nice."

"Well, it looks like you're making some positive changes."

"Hmm." I shrug my shoulders, not agreeing or disagreeing. I just want to stay inside my head. I lean forward, open the container of fish food, and drop some flakes into the bowl.

"How about your use?"

"My use? It's fine," says Echo. "I set my goals in school. On the weekends, I drink a little. But just weed during the week. I'm just kind of laying low."

Eric normally doesn't talk to me much about drugs, at least in terms of what I'm using. He says he'd rather talk about the issues surrounding my use, the things that probably make me want to use in the first place. So we talk about what stresses me out.

"And how's it going with your mom?"

"Same. Same. We've spent a little more time together."

Eric moves in his chair, straightens up slightly, and recrosses his legs. He does this when I say something right. He puts his finger to his lips and taps, as if trying to coax the words out of me.

"I don't want to talk about her."

His finger goes down. "Okay. So, we have twenty minutes left. What would you like to talk about?"

I shrug my shoulders. "I don't know."

"You want to pick a card?" he asks, motioning to this little plastic file box filled with index cards that have provoking questions on them. You're allowed to pass if you don't want to answer the one you get, so it's not a bad idea to get your mind thinking about something random and different.

"Sure." I open the box and choose a card from the middle. I read it aloud. "'Who owes you an apology?' Pass," I say quickly, and put the card at the back of the box. I know who that would be. My father. Wherever he is. Whoever he is. I take another. "'What was the worst day of your life?'"

Surprisingly, I keep this one. I hold it in my hand and tap it on the table as I think aloud about my answer. "That one is easy. The day Bradley died." I look up to the ceiling and think about other options: our first night in the shelter; the day my mom got beat up by her shithead boyfriend and the cops had to break down our door; the day I got my first grade-nine failing mark; the day my friend Meagan told me she had been raped by this guy in her neighbourhood. So many. "There's a few to choose from, but so far I'd say, yep, the day he died. For sure."

"Okay. Go ahead," he says, leaning back in his chair like I'm about to tell him a story.

"Well. I actually wasn't there at the hospital. I was in school. The principal came to get me out of class. Everyone went 'Ooooooo!' like I was in trouble, but then she told me to get my coat, and as I was walking down the hall with her, I had an idea it was about Bradley, because at this point he really wasn't doing well. She didn't say anything to me. She just said my auntie was here to pick me up. My auntie was my mom's friend Maureen, who's since moved to Arizona, but I used to call her auntie because she was always around. I could tell by the look on her face that it was bad. She was wearing sunglasses and in the car she kept dabbing under the glasses with a tissue. You know how people do that when they're crying?" I ask Eric.

He nods his head.

"I was so scared, I didn't want to ask. I just started to cry the closer we got to the hospital, and by the time we got to the underground parking, I was really bawling. She never did tell me he died—I just knew. When we went up to the room, Bradley wasn't in it. I remember being upset because I didn't get to say goodbye to him. They wouldn't let me. I remember my mom squatted on the floor in the corner, under the window, her head buried in her knees. She didn't move for a long time. Even when I came to hug her, she didn't lift her head. Her body just jerked and jerked and trembled, and her breathing was so heavy, and her reaction made me so, so …" I stare at the table for a while before I can find the right word. "… terrified. More terrified than knowing Bradley was gone. I remember holding on to her, hunched awkwardly over her shoulder and back, and then at some point I must have let go, because I remember being down in the cafeteria with my auntie eating macaroni and cheese.

"It was night when we went back to the room. Bradley's bags were packed. His father, Stewart, who used to come around to see him every other weekend, was there. I think he was the one loading the car with Bradley's stuff. And my mom was sitting now, on the bench she used to sleep on. And she looked at me with the most hollow, dead face. And I'll never forget that look, because I can still see it in her eyes. It's like since that day she's been a different person. Half dead. Half alive. Like nothing was ever important anymore, including me." I pause and then lay the index card flat on the table. "I guess our family sort of died that day too," I add, staring down at the card.

"Mmmmm," Eric says, as if he's eaten something yummy. "That's powerful, Melissa. Thanks for sharing that."

I look at him. "No problem." I pick the card up again and put it at the end of the box.

He continues, "I'm sorry you had to go through such pain when you were so young. And losing your brother—that's just not fair."

I nod my head. "Yeah. It's okay. It was a long time ago," I say, 'cause I want him to shut up now because I feel like I'm going to cry.

Eric goes on to say a few more things, about mourning, losing a family member, holding on to memories—stuff I easily tune out. Blah blah blah. It's only the last bit that I really listen to: "Seeing a parent, someone who protects you, as vulnerable or distressed can be earth-shattering to a child. Sometimes it can crack open that protective shell you've had surrounding you and hatch you into real life too quickly."

I like the way he said it. I've seen broken eggs with mangy, unformed birds inside them on TV. *Hatched into real life.* That's good. That's exactly how I felt. Like my shell was suddenly whacked against an edge and out I spilled, little bits of wet feather and bones, not yet ready for the life I was about to be flung into. I nod my head again. "Yeah. After that happened, things pretty much sucked."

Eric puts his hands together as we wrap up. "Well, on that positive note, shall we end it?" he says sarcastically.

I laugh a little.

"I'm just looking at the time now. It's been over seventy-five minutes," he explains.

I turn my head to the clock on the wall. "Whoa. That went fast."

I'm in a good mood when I leave. I don't know why, since what we talked about was so depressing. It's times like these that make me realize that Eric knows what he's doing after all. I can talk about seemingly random stuff and somehow he puts it all together, and in the end I feel a little better, without having a clue why or how.

Twenty-One

Zeus's punishment of Sisyphus at first seems comparatively kind and gentle. It didn't involve fire or serpents or destruction. While Gods and mortals battled it out around him, people getting murdered and kidnapped and beheaded, there was Sisyphus, bound to his quiet task of rolling the rock up the hill.

He just kept trying.

Up, up, up.

Until it was time to go down, down, down.

⟿

Uncle Freestyle says that when the sun rises, the hungry lion knows he must catch the slowest gazelle or starve. When the gazelle rises, he knows he must run fast to escape the lion. Whether you are a lion or a gazelle, when the sun rises, you better be running.

Go to school
Do my homework

Pass my tests
Take on more work hours
Eat
Be nice to people
Stop chemicals

This is my list of goals that my teacher, Ms. Dally, made me do.

It should be easy, but I don't know how normal kids do it. Do they try hard in school for the good marks? For the praise from their parents? Or because of the guilt? Do they attend classes because they actually like it? When they sit down to do homework, is that all they see in front of them—their homework? I just don't get it.

I try to be normal. I clean off the kitchen table before dinner, sharpen my pencil, and open up my textbook. My eyes stare at the page. It's torture. School work is part of some alien world. There's no intensity in it. It's just "doing." And I'd rather be high or answer the phone or fight with my mother. There's this whole chaotic world swirling in my mind while I stare at these tidy textbook pages and try to learn about soil profiles and dangling participles and factoring equations and *Je suis, Tu es, Il est*. And I just can't bring myself to that clean, lined-paper calm. It's like standing in the middle of a hurricane and someone passes you a book and asks you to recite poetry. And you're just, like, what the fuck? I can't do this now. Don't you see what's happening around us?

⟵

I try. I really, really try.

I spend two weeks going to school and I work on the weekends. I only smoke dope—no chemicals, drinking, pills, or coke. I take extra shifts at the clinic so that when Ally calls, I tell her I'm too tired to go out.

But being sober all the time is boring. That's just a plain fact. So is chilling at home. There are only so many movies you can watch, books you can read, only so many times you can listen to music, before you just feel like you're rotting away. And when you get bored, it's like falling into this sucking, trapping black hole that swallowed all the shit you usually successfully avoided thinking about when you're busy or stoned. And then you're stuck down inside all that guck, and it's awful.

So I try to keep out of that hole by doing sober things. I decorate my bedroom wall with magazine photos, creating a huge floor-to-ceiling collage. I finish a book almost every two days. And I decide to get an early start at making the animals' Christmas toys for work. Christmas is my favourite time to be at the clinic. It's also a good way to get out of spending all day cooped up with my mom and Crystal and Freestyle and whatever assorted boyfriend my mother has at the time. I have a good excuse to leave the apartment for a few hours in the afternoon, and when I come back everyone is so drunk they barely notice my return. I started the tradition two years ago, when I began volunteering. I make little presents for every animal that has to stay in the hospital, whether they are sick or just abandoned by their families who've gone on fancy vacations. And on Christmas Day I borrow Freestyle's stupid Santa hat, jingle some bells, and go cage to cage to give each animal its gift.

I can't predict exactly how many dogs, cats, rabbits, and whatnot there will be, so I start my sketch ideas in October and make at least ten toys by December so I have enough time for the last-minute bird or guinea pig toy. This year I decide that cats will get sock gifts. Giovanni gives me a plastic bag full of his old socks and I mess up the living room for a week, making "sneaky peaky serpents." I put two jingly rubber cat toy balls at either end and tie them in place. I also tuck a little catnip inside, just to keep them interested. Then I sew on two buttons at each end, like taunting eyes, and I attach a long red twisting pipe cleaner for a tongue.

Making the toys keeps me busy for about a week. But then I'm bored again and the thoughts come flooding in, about Michael, or about my mom, or about us not having enough money and why the fuck I'm so angry all the time, and I'm so close to just opening the kitchen cupboard and starting on a bottle of vodka.

I'm so pathetically antsy that I go to a movie with Rachel 'cause I know I won't get into trouble with her. She's been asking me to go out a few times, mentioning we should do something after work. We get along well enough. We have some laughs. So finally I mention this movie and we make plans to go after our Friday shift. We drive in her fancy white Mini and I feel like royalty, not having to take the bus.

Rachel is giggly and bubbly and so publicly happy it's embarrassing. Nauseating, really. She makes such a point of having fun that I don't want to have fun. I don't know what it is. It's as if being around someone really happy just makes me more mad. She takes my arm in hers as we go up the escalator. She texts her friends a thousand times. She insists on playing a game of pinball. She's not nerdy or naive. She's just ... I don't know. Clean?

We buy popcorn and drinks and sit in the back row. She immediately puts her feet up on the back of the seat in front of her, and when the lady to the left complains about it, she doesn't take them off, which surprises me. Impresses me, I suppose.

While we wait for the previews, Rachel insists on giving me a hand massage. She's taking a shiatsu course at her mother's wellness centre and says it's her homework to practise two hours of massage on people this week. I will be her last fifteen minutes. I reluctantly give her my hand. It seems a little strange, two girls holding hands. It's like we're lesbians or something. But I don't say anything, because in these situations it's more embarrassing to admit it's embarrassing. And in the end it's actually pretty good, and I feel myself relax into the seat a little more. My hand becomes this floppy, boneless mush that she prods and pulls and pokes, and I laugh a little to myself, because if one of my friends saw me now, they'd piss themselves laughing.

At the end of the night, she drops me off at a convenience store a few blocks away from my home because I don't want her to see where I live. It's partly because I don't want her to get all clingy and show up unannounced, and also because I don't want her to see my crappy apartment. In her chipper voice she tells me she had fun and that we should do it again. I say, "Yeah." But I'm just so happy to get out of the car because I find her totally boring. And I can't imagine living like this forever: not partying, just going to movies and living life sober.

Twenty-Two

My mom has been trying to turn things around too. She has a new boyfriend named Scott. *Current* boyfriend, that is. As in, *tonight*. This one seems okay. He's a Suit. That's what she calls him. Which already puts him miles ahead of any man she's ever brought around here. He's an accountant at the firm where she's been temping. Just got divorced. Probably on the rebound with my mom, but that's okay. As long as they're not assholes and don't play stepfather, I'm fine. And as long as they make my mom happy, I couldn't really care less.

After only three weeks of dating, Scott takes my mom and me away for the weekend to a resort in the country. I sit in the back of his BMW SUV and watch a DVD on the screen hanging from the roof, while my mom keeps going on about the brilliant colour of the fall leaves, like she's seventy years old and this is her first trip out of her home in years. It's like she's never seen a tree before.

We stay in our very own little house, with two bedrooms, a living room, a kitchen, and a deck. It overlooks the lake. The bathrooms have fancy soaps and shampoos and lotions. My room has its own personal balcony.

"Look at the reflection of the leaves in the water!" I shout from the deck, sounding now like my mom. But it truly is amazing, that watery fire of red and orange and yellow.

We are this instant little family. The Suit's family. We're like dolls he's playing house with. My mom and I go along with this pretend world 'cause we both know it won't last. We go hiking, mountain biking, and swimming in the indoor pool. My mom and I get facials at the spa while Scott plays squash with some guy. We get dressed up for dinner and walk to the dining room, where we have the fanciest, most expensive meal ever.

I excuse myself to go to the washroom but instead go outside for a quick smoke. When I return, Scott and my mom have ordered another bottle of wine and I get the feeling I should cut out. As I walk back to the table, I see them as if they were any other normal couple in the lodge. My mom looks nice in her black dress and all made up. And Scott, well, he looks like Scott, the way any man in a suit would look.

"I'm gonna go back to the house," I say, standing by the table instead of sitting down. I like saying that word, "house."

"What are you going to do?" my mom asks.

"I don't know. Sit by the water. Watch a movie. There's a pool table below the restaurant."

"Okay. Have fun, Hon. There's stuff in the fridge. But don't drink the beer. Maybe two, but no more. I'm going to count —"

"She shouldn't be drinking beer," Scott interjects, but then is silenced by my mom's evil glare.

"Relax," I say to both of them. "I don't want the beer. I don't even like beer."

Scott reaches into his pocket and gives me twenty bucks, but I'm embarrassed to take it.

"What does she need that for?" my mom asks, as if she's embarrassed too.

"I don't know. Maybe something from the candy machine."

"If he wants to give it to me, I'll take it," I say, stuffing the money in my pocket and glaring at my mom. It feels good to finally have someone on my side. It feels right.

I wander downstairs to the "teen room," where some rich guys my age are playing pool with what looks like their little sisters. The second I appear in the doorway, I regret going down. It's like this depressing games room with a stupid jukebox playing hip-hop. And the nerdy guys think they're so cool with their backward caps and boxer shorts sticking out of their jeans that are forty sizes too big for them. I just can't stand guys my age. They're so boring. Especially the rich ones who try to look all ghetto. I head to the lake to blaze before going back to the house.

I decide to walk across the sloping lawn spotted with iron post lights, toward the water's edge and along the beach. I don't have a good mid-season coat, so I'm just wearing my hoodie over the dress I wore to dinner. There's an older couple down there, wearing matching puffy sport vests like they're right out of a Gap ad. They smile at me in a way that no old people ever smile at me in the city. It's a nice smile. Like a look-at-the-sweet-young-girl-taking-a-stroll-in-the-moonlight smile. Like just because I'm in this ritzy place, suddenly I'm not a punk. And I should be pissed off at how superficial they are, but it feels good to be trusted by a stranger. Almost makes me feel like being trustworthy. Almost.

I continue walking. It's so black and quiet. It's a little cold, but not so bad for this time of year. I find a Muskoka chair that's off on its own. I light my joint and sit, just watching the moon and stars shimmering in the water. A loon calls in the distance. It's the most romantic place I've ever been, and of course all I think about is Michael. I want him here so, so badly. But being at this resort with Scott makes me realize that Michael was more than just a good boyfriend. He was about the life I wanted to have, the one I always dreamed of. A normal life. A house. A family. A career. And so losing Michael is more than just losing someone I love. It's like losing hope.

I reach up my hand to my mouth, close my eyes, and give it sloppy kisses. It's a pathetic replacement, but I can almost convince myself I feel him … his warm mouth pulling at my bottom lip, then the top, then both. I want to disappear right into that mouth, first my lips, then my face, then my neck, then all of me. We used to kiss for hours. Sometimes that was all we'd do. Then sometimes his hand would reach down to my belly and up into my shirt. And the next morning my boobs would be full of purple and red hickeys. And I loved those bruised kisses that lingered for days. So all I'd have to do when I missed him was lift open the top of my shirt and look down.

Now I wish he had stained all of me. I wish every kiss he ever gave had left a mark on me forever.

Twenty-Three

I'm lying on a towel on the small beach beside the lake, eating my picnic sandwich and watching my mom and Scott, who are lying on a big towel a few feet away. There are no other guests around. Maybe they think it's crazy to be on a beach at the end of fall, but it's a really hot day, warm enough to wear just a long-sleeve shirt. In the morning, my mom joked that it was so hot she wanted to wear her pink bikini. She paraded around the living room in it, saying she'd get her last tan in before the winter comes. I knew she was only doing it to show off her wicked body. She's thin and curvy in all the right places, while my body is just one fleshy flat line all around the perimeter, like a big rectangle.

I'm relaxed because I just smoked a joint behind the shack where they keep the canoes. I feel like a whole different person, no worries, just loving the heat of the sun on my face. It's like I'm not even myself, like I'm being filmed for a movie or something. And I'm totally happy, mostly because my mom is happy. It works that way. I wish it didn't. But I've lived long enough to know it's true.

If I were honest with myself (which is what happens when I'm high), I'd say I really want my mom to marry Scott. It's selfish, but if it happened, all our problems would go away. We wouldn't have to worry about money and I wouldn't have to worry about my mom all the time. Then I could just be a kid and do normal kid things. I think of myself in a bedroom with pink walls. I'd take figure skating lessons. We'd have a family dinner each night and someone would ask me if my homework was done. I'd have real dessert with whipped cream, and a curfew, and I'd study for exams.

I know that if this actually happened, I'd probably hate my life. I'd find it totally boring and fuck it all up, because it's like it's too late for me now. But who knows? Maybe after some time I'd get into it.

Some kind of bug lands on my neck and stings me. "Agghhh!" I shout, and slap my hand down hard. "Bitch!" I shout some more, really annoyed now, and then look back to my mom and Scott, who don't even turn to see what the problem is.

Then it's as if reality settles in, and I sober up. I shake my head, pissed off at the dumb fairy tale I was constructing. It was a stupid thought and I am an idiot for even letting myself get so far into the idea.

"I'm cold, I'm going," I announce, standing up and shaking the sand off my ass. I friggin' hate sand.

"Yeah. Okay." My mom waves absent-mindedly and goes back to her deep conversation with Scott. With nothing else to do, I decide to head back to the room and drink a beer. I don't even like beer, but I'll do anything just to shut my mind up.

Twenty-Four

It's always a little bit awkward when I walk into Eric's office. It's hard to shift gears from thinking about nothing to thinking about something. I spend every day just trying to forget how I really feel and then I have to face it all when I see him.

"Hey," I greet him, toss my backpack onto one of the empty chairs, and unzip my jacket.

"Hey yourself. Good timing—I just walked in. How's it going?" Eric takes off his own coat and puts down a Starbucks cup on the table.

"Okay," I answer, sit down, pick up two stress balls that are in a basket on the table, and start to juggle them while Eric puts away a folder and finishes writing a number on a yellow sticky note. He makes some small talk about stuff—school and my work—before he brings up what he really wants to discuss.

"So, how was the weekend away?"

"Actually, it was really good." I try to toss the balls up and down in one hand. One of them goes flying down to the floor and I'm too lazy to get it, so I just lean back and start squeezing the other one in my hands.

"You sound surprised."

"I am. I didn't think I'd like it."

"Hmmm … I'm glad. You like Scott?"

"Yeah. I can't really complain. Which feels weird. I guess part of me wants to hate him. And I guess I wanted to have a terrible time."

"Why's that?"

"'Cause it would be a lot easier than getting hurt in the end. It's obvious Scott and my mom aren't going to stay together. He's rich and has a nice house. And he's all proper and polite. And this perfect little life we have with him is just borrowed. I mean, you just can't go from a shitty apartment and living in a shelter to some mansion in Rosedale. It doesn't work like that, even though my mom promised, one day, we'd have a home. A real home, you know?"

"I'm sure she meant it when she said it."

"Yeah. I remember exactly when she said it. We were in the shelter after Bradley died. We were sitting in our crappy room, on the bed."

"That's right, you were there a couple of months. What was that like?"

"It was okay. We slept in a dorm room with something like ten beds. There were a couple other kids in there, but no men. Only women." I close my eyes and start to move around the room I see in my mind. "There were bunk beds, and me and my mom had two lower bunks side by side. In between us was a table we could put our stuff on. And a little cupboard underneath the table we could lock and keep some clothes in. We had to change in there with everyone else around. It was really awkward. But what was most terrible was sleeping. Hearing everyone breathe and snore and fart. And sometimes I heard my mom crying. That was the worst. I remember that really scaring me." I pause a second, because I hadn't thought of all this in such a long time and it's weird how real it still feels to me. "I remember waking in the dark, really late, and always hearing the radio playing down the hall, at the security desk. There was never total silence. Which probably should have been comforting, but actually was kind of creepy."

I open my eyes again. "The worst was the toilets. There was an open shower area, without any drapes. Just a few shower pipes with, like, five shower heads around each one, so all the women had to stand naked in little circles. It was really gross. It was the first time I saw women's bodies." The recollection makes me shudder.

"Where did you eat?"

"In the cafeteria. It was a big room with longish tables. We usually sat alone or with a friend of my mom's, who also had a kid who was a few years younger than me that I got stuck basically babysitting while they talked. There was a playroom. I remember that being cool, even though I was too old for it. I'd colour, and play this game with marbles. A lady used to play with me. She was young. I think she was a volunteer. One time I made chocolate chip cookies with her in the kitchen."

"So you've described what it looked like. What about the general feel of the place?"

"I don't know …" I try to think about being twelve again. Imagine myself walking around the place. "I don't really remember being sad. I was more worried about my mom. The place itself wasn't awful. It's only later, when I got older, that I put negative feelings into the memories. It's like at the time, it just *was*. There were always people around, you know? And nothing was ours—not the sheets or the pillows or even the soap. But it wasn't that bad. It was more the idea that no one wanted to be there that made it depressing. I guess if it was a place people *wanted* to go, it would have been fine. But since it was a shelter and no one wants to be in a shelter, it was like reality turned everything a certain grey and you couldn't see the colour." My lips stop moving and it's as if I've just returned to the room after being far away in my mind. "Oh," I remark, "I've been talking a lot."

"It's okay. That's what we're here for."

"My mouth is tired."

Eric laughs. "Then let's give it a rest, shall we?"

Twenty-Five

I try to pretend to myself that I've stopped thinking about Michael. I pretend to everyone that things are fine, but inside I'm really dying. Each morning I wake with the hope that maybe today he will call. And each night I go to bed, sad that he didn't. When I can't sleep, I lie in the dark and go over every single second we ever spent together, from beginning to end. I play it like a movie in my head, so I even see myself in the scenes. Then sometimes I imagine him calling me.

"Hi."

"Michael?"

"Yeah. Hi."

"Hi."

"I know you're mad, but I'm coming back for you."

"You are?"

"Yeah. Not now. In two years. I love you, Melissa. I want to be with you forever. Wait for me. When you're eighteen, I'll be there."

"Eighteen? That's so long. Why eighteen? It's just a number. I can't wait. I might be dead by then."

"You won't be dead. You're too strong, baby. We're going to be together. I know it."

"But if you love me, how can you be away from me?"

"I need to get my shit together. You need to get older. If we're together now, we won't last."

"Yeah, maybe it's true. But I can't be alone so long. You have to come back."

"I will."

"I don't think I can wait so long."

"Wait, baby. Wait. I will wait for you …"

And it goes on and on like that. But I wonder how long *I* can go on like this — waking with hope, falling asleep in tears. It feels endless, but I suppose it's bound to stop. One day I'm bound to wake without the thought of Michael beside me in my bed. Aren't I?

Twenty-Six

The minute I swear off men, I meet someone remotely interesting. His name is Fortune, he's nineteen, and he's so incredibly gorgeous it's almost impossible not to want to jump him. He's got a baby face, beautiful brown skin, short dreads, and the most amazing body. "It's as if he puts sexy into every movement," Jess says. Hot, hot, hot! He'll be standing in front of you then suddenly reach up over his head to stretch, revealing his six-pack stomach. Or he'll lean one arm up on the fridge door at a party, deciding for the longest time on what beer to take, while all the girls in the room stare at his fine ass.

I've seen him around before. I always thought he was cute, but it was obvious he was a player, so I didn't consider him. He's the kind of guy who makes girls fall in love with him, gets what he can out of them, and moves on. *Any* girl—Chinese, black, Hispanic, brown, anything. Even the guys are drawn to him. He always has a permanent posse of wannabes hanging around.

But on Saturday night, at Jasmyn's friend's friend's place, here Fortune is, beside me on the couch, treating me like I'm the only girl in the room. His thigh pressed against mine. His sexy voice up close in my ear, so close I feel his cheek against mine. I'm so fucked up on some stuff Jasmyn gave me to snort that I decide to tolerate him. He is telling me I'm different than the other girls. He is telling me he's been watching me a long time.

"That's bull," I argue.

He laughs. "You see? You're smart. I like that. You don't let me get away with shit and I barely know you." He reaches his arm around me, resting his hand against my tit as if it's unintentional. "You walk around like you don't care about anyone. Like you're a dyke or something. Your friend Allison kind of looks like a dyke. What's up? Are you a carpet muncher?"

I slap him in the chest. "No!"

"You sure?" He puts his hand back again.

"Is this why you prey on sixteen-year-olds? Because they buy this shit?" I pull away firmly this time.

"Hah!" He laughs. "Usually."

⤺

I don't know how it all happens, but Fortune drives me home and we end up messing around in his black BMW E36 with tints and blackout grilles. He blasts 2Pac on his sweet boomin' system. I feel the vibrations in the seat. He apologizes for the apparently indecent sound quality. "I got a blown sub and I'm gonna put in a Pioneer 500-watt ten-inch Fosgate," he says. I have no idea what he's talking about.

We pull into the parking lot out back of my building for a while. We don't have sex because I have my period. His phone rings a thousand times, and he answers it no matter what we're in the middle of doing. His conversations are the same: "Yeah.

Right. Twenty. Fifty. Yeah." And I know he's dealing, which makes me like him even more, because it means he's got a brain.

"See ya, babe," he says when we're done, giving me this most luscious kiss.

"Yeah. Later," I say, shutting the door. Then he pulls away, without giving me his number.

I go up to my room, lie in bed, and think of him. I think of his lips. His hair. His smooth skin. His biceps. His thighs. His fingers.

I feel sort of guilty about Michael, but part of me wants to hurt him for leaving me. And when he comes back, I want him to think I moved on so he'll be jealous and see how good a catch I really am. But for tonight, even if I am drunk, I feel happy, and it's just so delicious to fall asleep with the thought of someone else for a change.

Twenty-Seven

Uncle Freestyle and I talk about the craziest things. Sometimes I really love him. He comes over every Monday night to watch football and we usually go out on the balcony at halftime and blaze. It's like our own little counselling office.

I tell my mom that I don't have to go see Eric, that Freestyle is just as good.

"That's insane," she says. "That man has no capacity for moral guidance. Look at his life." She's talking about his three kids with three different women. And his smoking pot. And his endless art projects that never get started. And his long string of home repair jobs.

"He says pretty smart stuff."

She looks at me in disbelief. "That's because you're a kid. You think everyone sounds smart."

"No I don't." I want to say I don't think *she* sounds smart. Or her friend Crystal. Or my CYC at school. But the thing is, Freestyle *is* super smart. When he was little, he skipped two grades. He got kicked out of high school, but he can play Jeopardy and get every question right. He's the one who taught me how to smoke poppers and to blow out the smoke through a toilet paper roll stuffed with Bounce sheets so my mom won't smell it. And he's this amazing painter. His stuff is so good, it could be in galleries.

I look carefully at my mother, thinking there must be more between them that I don't know. "Why do you hate him so much?"

She rolls her eyes. "We're related. That's what brothers and sisters do—they hate each other."

"Bradley and I didn't hate each other."

"No." She smiles warmly. "You didn't hate each other. You were too young. You probably would have later, though."

⌒

When I tell Freestyle out on the balcony that he should be a counsellor to teenagers, he says he's got enough problems of his own, that he wouldn't want to sit around and listen to other people's issues all day. To make conversation, I end up telling him about my weekend. I always tell him what's up with my friends, and which guys I've been with. He doesn't like hearing about the sex that much, but he doesn't get all fatherlike about it. This time I tell him about Fortune.

"He's black?"

"No, he's orange. Yeah. So?"

He shrugs his shoulders.

"What, you from the Dark Ages? What's wrong with a black guy?"

"Nothing."

He annoys me a little. How can he be so cool yet sometimes so ignorant?

"You on the pill?"

"Yeah. Sort of. I have this thing in my arm. Mom made me get it."

"Good." He switches his tone. "So, why do you think you're with so many guys?"

"I'm not with 'so many guys,'" I say defensively.

"Enough guys …"

"I don't know. Yeah, maybe. But once you start, it's like, 'Why not?'" Then I tell him what I always tell Eric: "It just feels good."

"Well. Hell! Yeah! Of course! Lots of things feel good. But that doesn't mean you have to always do it. Sure, sex is excellent, hot … but it doesn't mean you screw every guy you see."

I get pissed at him. "I don't!"

His silence is his objection. It pisses me off. If we were done our joint, I'd go back in. I fold my arms and wait for him to pass me the last bit.

"What do you think the guys say about you?"

"What do you mean?" I ask, knowing full well what he means.

"You think they respect you, or do they think you're trash?"

I laugh.

"No, I'm serious. You think they talk about you?"

I shrug my shoulders. "I don't know. And I couldn't care less if they did."

"You would if you heard what they said."

I start to get angry. "How do you know what they say? What do you know?"

"I know guys. I was your age, and I'm still a guy. I definitely know guys."

"Well, I don't fuckin' care what they say. I do what I want to do."

"Well, I'll tell you this: they don't respect a girl who's with everyone. They might be nice to your face, but they say shit to each other about you. And I don't see any of them wanting to be your boyfriend."

Now I get really mad. "Shut up."

"I'm just saying it like it is, Melissa."

We're quiet for a bit. I'm too mad to talk and he's probably trying to find a way to end a pathetic conversation on a positive note. I consider telling him about Michael, but it would only be for me to prove a point. And in the end I know I'd regret it, 'cause he'd just get pissed about how old he is and get all worked up about wanting to go find him and kick his ass.

"I'm just saying, Melissa, that there's a reason you're doing it." His voice changes to this caring tone. "And if you have sex with so many guys—"

I contest, "Not *so* many!"

He lights a new joint and passes it over. "So, anyway, the question is, what do you think you get out of it?"

"Now you're really sounding like my counsellor," I say, taking the joint and inhaling.

I stand there awhile, staring at the red embers and thinking about it. He's right. Damn, he's smart sometimes. There must be something more. I don't do it to get a boyfriend, like Shayla does. And it's not like I don't feel pretty enough to get a guy so I have to be a slut, like Allison. So what is it?

"I guess I like that I'm good at it," I conclude, not really satisfied with my own answer. I turn and look directly at him. "Why do *you* like it?"

He laughs and then lights up a cigarette. "I never said I liked it."

"Whatever. You have three kids."

He doesn't respond, so I let it drop. Like me, Freestyle has a short attention span, and once he's done with a topic, it's done. He turns and looks in through the window to check the TV. "Those goddamn cartoon beavers on those commercials. Are they faggots or what? Let's go in. It's cold out here."

Twenty-Eight

I usually take the codeine pills from work, just two or three a week. Just enough to keep me going on the boring Saturday and Sunday afternoons when I've partied all night and want to crash the next day. I can never really sleep. Not fully, because the E or the coke or whatever is still pulsing in my blood. So I put on a DVD, close the curtains, get under a bunch of blankets on the couch, and pop a pill.

The pills don't make me feel high, just *cozy*. And it means I don't have to worry about my mom, hungover in the next room with whoever she's with. Or about my neighbour screaming. Or about my friend Sid knocking on the front door with a pocketful of weed and a hard-on in his pants.

I watch a cockroach creep across the table. This place is a dump. I should clean it. Michael's apartment was a dump too, but he's a bachelor, so that's different. His place looked just like the guys' places where I hang out on the weekends: messy, clothes on the floor, old pizza boxes stacked under the kitchen table, empty beer bottle boxes by the back door. Except he had books. Lots and lots of books, everywhere.

I liked picking up his shirts and folding them in a pile, even though I hate doing the same thing in my own house. My mother and I have fought endlessly about my laziness. At home, with my own stuff, I just don't care. But at Michael's, it's like I wanted to clean the bathroom and take out the garbage and remove the bins from the fridge and rinse them down. It's insane. I became a cleaning lady when I was at his place. Not because it disgusted me or because I wanted him to be impressed, but I think because I just wanted to take care of him. And that's such a weird feeling, I can't explain it.

⌐→

I hear Scott's voice inside my mom's bedroom. They're fighting. Their voices are somewhat muffled, but I can hear enough to know that Scott is pissed off about something my mother did, probably something stupid. Scott puts my mom straight. He doesn't let her dick him around. She needs that. Someone strong and reasonable.

"I'm not your prisoner!" she yells, storming out of the room. She's wearing a tight pink tank top and my blue boy short underwear that hangs loose on her.

"Hey, I've been looking for those!" I shout from under the covers, only to be drowned out by Scott's bellowing voice.

"Then don't have strange numbers on your phone! If there are no strange numbers, then you wouldn't have to look!"

My mother storms back to the bedroom doorway. "I have friends, you know! I'm allowed to have friends."

"Not if you're fucking them, you're not!"

Oooooo! I pull up the blanket to hide my smile. He's totally right. Smart man. My mom does have fuck-friends. Everyone knows this. She's a classic hustler, only she's a woman. She tells men what they want to hear, gets what she wants out of them, and plays them off against each other. Even *she* calls herself a cougar.

"Go to hell!" she shouts.

"Do you mind?" I shout, because I don't like her being such a bitch to Scott. "I'm trying to watch a movie!"

My mom turns her head to the mound of blankets on the couch and sees my blazed eyes looking out. "Sorry, I didn't see you." She pauses a moment and does a double take, like she knows I'm in a medicated daze, but then she heads back into the room and closes the door behind her. The shouting continues. I turn up the volume so loud the TV vibrates and tickles my ears, and I start to laugh.

⤝

That night, I make a point of saying something to my mom about Scott, because, despite my sleepy fog, I actually worried about them all day. It seems I'm always worrying about my mom, and I'm getting real tired of it. Worrying when she'll break. Fall apart. Fuck up. Get drunk. Get depressed. Crawl into her cave to hibernate because things are getting rough, leaving me to take care of everything.

"Don't screw this up, Mom," I say to her after she gets off the phone from talking to him, seemingly like everything is fine again.

"What does that mean?" she asks defensively, ready for a fight.

"Nothing. Just don't go all crazy or get him jealous."

"Thanks for the vote of confidence," she snaps.

"Well … it's not like I don't talk from experience."

She doesn't say anything back. Probably 'cause she knows I've got a lot on her, and that there's no way she could win this argument. She starts to tidy up the kitchen a bit and then finishes a half-eaten orange that's been lying on the counter since yesterday.

"Anyway …" I let her off the hook. "I like him."

My mom steps into the kitchen doorway, wipes her mouth with a napkin, and smiles. It was a rare confession of approval on my part. "You do?"

I smile. Suddenly the mood is lighter. I like that about me and my mom: we can say shit to each other one minute, then be nice the next. "Yeah. So like I said, don't screw it up."

She walks past me and tosses her crumpled napkin at my head. "Shut up," she says playfully, and continues on to her room.

Twenty-Nine

He's never going to call.

I can't eat.

I'm always on the verge of tears.

He never said it for certain. Michael never came out and said, "We're finished."

Is it because he didn't want to completely leave me?

I'm beginning to think that limbo is worse than heaven or hell.

The in-between.

I'm somewhere in between being in love and having my heart destroyed. I'm trapped in a waiting room, not permitted to feel bliss or misery. It's like knowing you won the lottery but not having the ticket in your hand. Or being given a death sentence by a doctor but forgetting to ask just how long you have left.

I lie on my bed and smoke joint after joint after joint. My mom is in the living room, but she doesn't mind me smoking ganja anymore, as long as I do it at home where she knows I'm safe. My mind drifts, soars, wafts, and squeezes through dark, pulsing tunnels, until I find myself in my no man's land, where every day I pace the muddied grass like a prisoner, back and forth. Caging me in are two rusty wire fences on either side. There are no trees. The sky is grey. It's chilly but not uncomfortable.

I stand still for a while, in the middle, waiting. I hear birds.

Then I walk over to one of the side fences. This is the side where Michael loves me still. When I'm here, I feel our love so strongly. I feel like I know what he's doing. He's giving us time, because if he stayed with me, we wouldn't last. He's waiting for me to grow up, and then he'll come back for me.

Next I wander over to the other side, where the grass is less worn. This is the side where misery lives. I can feel Michael's ghost here. He's gone. Beyond this fence is winter: hard, icy, windswept snow that blends into an indistinguishable white sky. I can bear it only for a few seconds before I panic, my chest constricts, and I can't breathe. I feel I'll collapse. I'd rather kill myself than disappear into that hopelessness.

Fuck you, Michael.

I need to know if I should wait for you or if you broke up with me.

I need an answer.

Now.

Thirty

The thought isn't in my mind when I enter Dr. Williams's office. At least, I don't think it is. But while I'm here looking for some gauze, the file cabinet catches my eye. I know from being in the office before that our employee records are kept in there. I had to fill out an employee information sheet when I was hired. On the sheet, I had to write down emergency contact information. It occurs to me that if Michael wrote down his parents' number, I could call them to get his new number and put an end to this waiting game.

The cabinet is locked, but a guy from school once showed me how to pick them, so I get a sharp knife from the kitchen and start jamming it in. It works.

Michael's file is near the front. I simply write his mom Mavis Butler's phone number down on a sticky note. But then I see the other stuff: his address, his resumé, his allergies. I want it all. Just to have it. So I take all the papers, fold them up, and put the whole bunch in my pocket. He isn't there anymore, so no one would be looking for any of it.

Everything is good until I try to lock the file cabinet back up and it won't go. A rush of panic spreads over me. I try to ram and jam the drawer in, wiggle and push the lock, but it still doesn't catch. I go back to the hallway to see if anyone is around, and then I give the drawer a few hard kicks.

"Hey!" A voice startles me. "What are you doing?" Rachel asks, appearing in the doorway.

I am relieved it's only her. "Here, help me. The lock is jammed."

She walks in, taking note of the knife on top of the cabinet. "What did you do, break it open?" She moves in, pushes my hand away, and tries to jimmy the lock.

"I already did that."

She starts ramming the drawer the way I was when she walked in.

I push her out of the way. Useless girl. I should never have asked her in the first place. "Shut up! Move!" I command, getting mad at myself for thinking she'd be any better at this than me.

"What were you doing?"

"Nothing."

"You jam a knife in a lock and it's nothing? What are you stealing?"

"Fuck!" I remark, frustrated with the drawer. "Nothing that concerns you."

She tries to help me again, but in the end we have to give up because it's too risky with staff around.

"Don't tell anyone," I warn her. It comes out as a threat.

"Obviously," Rachel snaps back.

We head back downstairs.

"What did you take?" she asks, following close behind me. "The petty cash?"

"No. A piece of paper."

"Paper? What kind of paper? Why would you steal a piece of paper?"

I want to tell her about Michael. If she knew I only wanted a telephone number, I wouldn't look like such a criminal. But I've been a little wary of Rachel lately. In fact, I've been suspicious of a lot of people at work. I know people can tell I smoke weed sometimes on my breaks. I can tell by the whispers. And they're not talking to me so much anymore. Even one of the veterinarians hinted I should get some perfume when I walked by her after smoking a blunt on a break.

"Just forget it. And don't tell anyone," I warn her.

Thirty-One

I sit on my bed and look at the script I've written out. I don't think I've ever been more nervous.

I cut class this morning so I could call Michael's mom from my room. My idea is to tell her I'm calling from the clinic. I'll say Accounting realized they owe him one more cheque and they have some questions to ask him before they process it. Then I'll get his number.

A woman answers the phone. "Hello?" It's strange to hear her voice. She sounds old. I imagine this anorexic lady with long brownish hair framing Michael's face.

I try to make my voice professional. "Yes. Hello. This is Becky Jarvis? I'm calling from Willow Animal Clinic, where Michael was employed? Accounting has noticed that they might owe him one more cheque? We are wondering if you could give us his number, so we could ask him some questions?"

"Oh," she says, pausing a moment. "Well. Michael isn't in town. He's away for a bit. I don't really have a number for him. But if I take your number, I can have him call you."

"Where is he?" I blurt out.

"He's in Chicago."

"Why is he there?" I ask.

"Pardon me?"

"I mean, he left so quickly. No one expected it ..."

"I'm sorry, what was your name again?"

Breathe. "Becky. From Accounting."

Her tone changes. "Becky. Let me take your number and he'll call you."

"Forget it," I say abruptly, and hang up.

⤣

Thoughts race through my mind. I was hoping he was in a coma somewhere. Or locked up in a mental institution. In jail, or maybe even dead. But Chicago is just a phone call away. Chicago is so close.

⤣

A thought occurs to me. They call it an *epiphany*, "a sudden intuitive leap of understanding." And just like the definition says, my epiphany truly *is* sudden. It's stark and sharp and takes my breath away. It *is* a leap, a plunge into a black reality ending with a skull-breaking smack against hard concrete when I land.

He's not coming back to me.

I sit on the floor, my back against the bed, cradle the phone in my lap, and curl over to bury my head in my arms. I feel my face contort and pull and squeeze. I don't know what I'm doing, something between a scream and a cry. My mouth is open, there are tears, but it's silent. And then ... a huge gasp of air and I let it all go. It seems impossible to shed so much water from a seemingly dry body.

I feel like I've broken more than my heart. A rib? A lung? A muscle in my jaw? A tear duct?

⌐

I'm more sad than I was the day I found out Michael left me. Because that day there was uncertainty. And that meant there was hope. A possibility of misunderstanding or misinterpretation or misinformation.

But now there is a clear answer.

⌐

After some time, I get up off my bedroom floor and wander aimlessly around the room. I don't know what to do. I walk over to my bed, then turn and walk over to my desk, then turn and walk over to my closet and then over to the window. I'm in a daze. My face feels numb and puffy.

Even though it's a crappy, grey, cold day, I decide to go outside for a walk. I just need to move, feel the cold on my face. I end up wandering down behind our building to sit by the play park and smoke a cigarette. I wish I had some weed.

It's an ugly time of year. The grass is brown. The trees are nearly all bare. There's practically no colour anywhere. Some young boys are standing at the top of the plastic cylinder slides taking turns pissing down the orange tubes. An old Indian lady, all gracious and sparkling in her sari that swells from underneath a thick ski jacket, sits on another bench with what I guess is her grandchild. There's pumping, vibrating music pulsing from a black car in the corner of the parking lot, windows tinted, motor running.

And then there's me, sitting in the middle of this scene, feeling scattered and so very small. I bring my feet up to rest on the bench and hold my knees tight.

⌐

I sit here for the longest time. People come and go. The sari lady eventually gets up and strolls the kid away. The black car tears off around the building. And I keep sitting here, not really thinking about much, other than how sorry I feel for myself.

Then, after the self-pity and my fifth cigarette, I finally get to the truth. I'm surprised about what is really making me upset. Because I realize that what kills me, what absolutely rips my soul apart, is not actually that I'll never see Michael again. It's the realization that Michael, even the mere thought of him, was what was helping me get by in this pathetic life.

And without Michael, without the dream of him, I have nothing.

Michael saved me.

He was like this unexpected gasp of breath above water before I submerged again. A second chance. But I'm beginning to think it wasn't a good thing. I'm beginning to think he just prolonged the slow dying. It would have been better to just let me drown.

I go sit on a swing beside some little girl who's swinging high, kicking her legs up and up, trying to fly like a bird. I think of Bradley and how I'd push him on a swing set just like that for hours. "Higher! Higher! Higher!" he'd shout. How I wish I was that young again.

It's hard to explain the presence of an absence. I wasn't aware that the idea of Michael was colouring everything for me, making life richer and more beautiful. It's only now that he's gone from my mind and I'm left to face the stark, bare, chilling reality that I see it for real …

My fucking ugly life.

I don't go home until after eleven 'cause I know I just end up fighting with my mom when I'm so upset. So I sit in the park and then go walking around the streets, thinking about stuff. At some point I feel calm enough to go to sleep, because I've made a decision about my life: I'm not giving up. I'm giving in. There's a difference. I give in to the destiny I'm being pushed toward. There's no point in changing. I give in to my shitty life with my shitty friends and my shitty future. But it's not a surrender; it's more like I'm stopping the resistance. Why fight it if you always lose in the end? Why believe in that little bit of hope? There are only so many times you can get knocked down before lying on the ground becomes more enticing than the fight.

Why was the Lady of Shalott cursed, anyway? They don't say what she did to deserve it. It's just a given that she's doomed to this life of solitude, and the story goes on from there. No one questions why. Sisyphus's mistake was clear: he didn't obey the gods. But it seems the Lady was just born into it. Like me.

Thirty-Two

Jasmyn arranges it so that I bump into Fortune again at one of her friends' parties. We see each other the moment I walk in the door. He's sitting on the couch, his arm up around some fat blond girl whose tits are hanging out of her shirt. He nods coolly in my direction, like I'm almost a stranger, and then turns back to the boobs.

I'm so pissed off and tell Jasmyn I'm not staying.

"Take it easy," she coaches. "He'll come to you. He likes you. Markus told me so. Just chill. Here." She passes me a beer from out of her backpack.

The whole night goes by and I talk to losers while Fortune hits on every girl in the room but me. I tell myself I don't care, but the more drunk I get, the more upset I am about it. At three o'clock, now thoroughly drunk, I tell Jasmyn I'm going to the washroom and then I'll be leaving.

After I'm done in the bathroom, I open the door and find Fortune's face right up in the crack. He smiles, all chilled. "Hey."

"Hey," I say coldly, and try to push the door open to leave, but he's holding it still. "You gonna let me out?"

"You gonna let me in?" He smiles so damn sexy I want to kill him.

"No. You fucking kidding me? Where is your girlfriend?"

He laughs. "Which one?"

"Yeah, exactly," I say, pushing harder on the door.

"I'm coming in," he warns, and pushes through, starts kissing me, and locks the door behind him. I'm so weak-willed, I don't even fight him off. "Oh, babe. I wanted to kiss you all night," he whispers.

I push him back. "You didn't even look at me once."

He ignores my comment and leans in to kiss again, hard this time. He wants me so badly, I feel it all over. It's like he can't get enough of me. And I'm so happy that he chose me. Of all the girls he could be with tonight, he chose *me*. And I'm going to make sure he knows he made the right choice. I welcome his warm, soft lips, and then his hands, and then he pulls down my jeans and underwear and lifts me onto the bathroom counter.

⌒

Later, when Fortune drives me home, he's like a different person, all mellow and sweet. He tells me about his family and I realize he's not as big a jerk as I wanted to think he was. Which is a damn shame, because it means I might end up liking him for real after all. He tells me he lives at home because he takes care of his mom and his little brothers, who are something like eight and ten. His mom is sick, she's got chronic fatigue syndrome, and he says sometimes she doesn't get out of bed for days. He's basically the father around his house, which for some reason he doesn't seem to mind. All that makes me like him even more.

Even though he gets all soft talking to me on the way home, he doesn't kiss me goodbye like last time. He basically just stops the car and keeps his hands on the steering wheel, like he's in a rush to go somewhere else. I pretend everything is cool, and tell him I'll see him around. I watch the reflection of his car lights in the lobby window as I walk away.

If I can't be with Michael, then I might as well be with Fortune. I promise myself that I'll try to give him a chance, even though my heart is somewhere else. And to be honest, it feels good to have someone wanting me.

Thirty-Three

Today was Bradley's birthday. It's probably why I've been thinking about him so much lately. He was cremated, so there's no grave to visit. Instead, we go every year to the park behind our old apartment complex, where he used to play. It's a few blocks away from where we live now, but we might as well just go outside our own home because all the apartment playground parks look the same, with the same rundown equipment and dirty gravel ground, as if a nuclear bomb had wiped out all trees, grass, and anything vibrant and just left behind a skeleton of metal.

We bundle up and sit on a bench. My mom sets up a framed photo of Bradley, her Discman and speakers in between us, and we have to listen to this sad Cat Stevens CD. I don't mind this tradition, but I don't understand why we can't celebrate his birthday in a restaurant or somewhere normal. It seems so morbid here in the park.

There are a few kids in the playground, running around, laughing and shouting and tripping over themselves. They are all about how old Bradley would have been, which makes the whole thing even sadder.

I try to lighten the mood by talking about something happy. "You remember that wacky ice cream truck with the hand-painted cones and soft drinks on the side? It would play that out-of-tune music?"

"Yeah." My mom smiles. "'The ants come marching two by two.'"

"And Bradley would go berserk. Jumping up and down, shouting, 'Ice cream! Ice cream!'"

"Ha!" my mom laughs, slapping her hand down to her thigh. "He was so damn excited, it was hard to say no."

"And he'd smear the chocolate all over his face …"

"I swear it was on purpose …"

"And I tried to smear it on my face once—"

"—until you saw that boy you had a crush on."

I whack my mom on the arm. "Did not! It just didn't feel good."

"Whatever," my mom teases.

I don't make a big deal about it, but she's wrong. I remember that day well. I remember the ice cream on my face because I was disappointed I couldn't just forget it was there. I remember being sad that I couldn't go back to the freedom of being a kid anymore.

We stop talking 'cause the memory is over and neither of us has anything left to say. My mom starts to raise a hand to her face and I know she's crying. I get tears too, but I hold them back. Afterward, we plant a chestnut tree seed somewhere in the barren field, because Bradley liked squirrels and chestnut trees. Usually after that we just head home and order something nice for dinner, like Swiss Chalet, but this time my mom says she wants to go back and sit on the bench again. So we do, and I wonder what's up. Until she speaks …

"Melissa, I'm pregnant."

"What?"

"About two months or so. I didn't know. That's why I've been feeling so rotten."

"Two months?" I'm trying to do the math. She's only been with Scott for about two months. "So whose is it?"

"I'm not exactly sure. Hopefully Scott's."

Hopefully? "Does he know?"

"No."

I don't go there. I don't want to know what will happen. The silence grows between us, and in its emptiness I place all the things that will go wrong. He will leave her. She will have a nervous breakdown. She will lose the baby. She will start drinking again. We will lose the apartment. My life will be fucked. I feel the anger rising up inside me.

"Well. Congratulations?" I ask.

"Don't be mad, Melissa."

"I'm not," I reply weakly, and scowl up to the sky. I just can't believe it. What kind of god is supposed to be up there?

Thirty-Four

A baby?

I don't talk to my mom for a week. I can't help it. I'm mad. How can she be so stupid? She can't handle a baby. She can barely take care of herself. I hate her growing belly. I hate her tired, lazy-ass body crashing on the couch early every night in front of the TV. I hate her pathetic voice when she talks to Crystal on the phone, telling her all her problems and woes, like she wants everyone to feel sorry for the choices she's made. She's so weak it makes me sick. I avoid going home. I spend a lot of time at Fortune's place, or I go to Jessica's or Ally's. Whoever's house I can crash at.

My mom buys fruits and vegetables and puts them in a big bowl on our kitchen table, and then comments on it every time someone comes over. "I'm on a health kick," she explains proudly, and I know she's dying to tell them about the pregnancy. But then she hides in her room and smokes cigarettes. She thinks I can't smell it. She thinks the incense she burns hides it. She thinks I'm as stupid as she is.

I feel sorry for her kid. I feel sorry for that little baby.

I wake up angry, every day, so I go to Jessica's place in the mornings before school to smoke a few joints because her mom goes to work early and she has the apartment to herself. Jess is usually who I go to if I want to talk about my mom, and Ally's for when I want to talk about guys. I sit on Jess's bed and roll the joints while she sits at this princess vanity table with bright lights all around the mirror, doing her hair and makeup. It takes her like an hour, and in the end she pretty much looks the same: plain Jane, except with a bit of shimmer around her eyes.

I light up the second joint, take a few drags, and then continue my thought. "I mean, how can she take care of a baby when she can't even take care of herself? She can't pay the rent herself—she needs a man to do it for her. But she can't keep a boyfriend. Can't even cook. I do everything for her. *Ev-er-y-thing.* I do laundry, make dinner. You know what? She doesn't even know how to clean an oven. You know what she did? She pushed the automatic cleaning button. She thought it would just clean itself. She's such an idiot."

"How's she gonna clean her baby's ass? Is she gonna push a button for that too?" Jessica starts laughing hysterically, like it's the funniest thing humankind has ever said. She can be nerdy when she's high. I roll my eyes and wait till she stops, because I know when she's laughing like that there's nothing you can do.

"Sometimes you're an idiot," I say.

Jess scowls. "What's your problem? What's the big deal, anyway? It's not like she's told you she's dying or something."

"'Cause I'm not taking care of a stupid baby." I move over to stand behind her, push her head to the side, and check out my own hair in the mirror. "I'm not changing one fuckin' diaper. I'm not picking it up from daycare. I'm not staying home every night shaking little jingly toys in front of its face. If I wanted to fuck up my own life, I would have had my own baby. Shit. Look. My hair looks terrible."

Jessica raises her eyes as if she's finally listening to me and carefully assesses my appearance in the mirror. "No it doesn't." She reaches for the hairspray. "Here. Close your eyes."

She doesn't just dab a little here and there, she lets it all go. I pull back. "Jesus Christ, Jessica! Spray my hair, not my face. Fuck!"

She starts laughing hysterically again. "Stay still, then."

"I wasn't even fucking moving," I snap, heading toward the washroom to rinse the sticky crap off my face. Afterward, instead of going back to her room, I just head out the front door. I don't say goodbye. Not because I'm angry about the hairspray, but because I'm just generally feeling pissed off. Even the ganja buzz doesn't soften my mood.

Thirty-Five

My anger is like a festering cancer that just grows and grows. Unfortunately for my mother, she's on the receiving end of it all. I don't know why I hate her so much. I can't really pinpoint any one thing, but for some reason she's the incarnation of all that makes me furious. Even little things will set me off, like when I'm sitting on the couch watching TV and I lift the converter to switch the channel and nothing happens. I smack the thing a few times, but still nothing happens.

"Fuck!" I yell, and whack the converter against the coffee table to shock it back to life. I try again. Nothing. "Fucking shit!" I yell, stomping my foot hard on the floor. I turn it over, open the back, and roll the batteries around a little, which sometimes helps. I try again. Still nothing. "Bitch!" I shout, and throw the converter across the room, where it hits the wall then rebounds and smacks one of Bradley's framed photos off the corner table.

My mother tears out of her room, her face all panicked. "What happened?"

"There are no fucking batteries in the converter!" I snap.

"For God's sake … then change them." Her face changes

from alarm to annoyance. She storms over to the table, sees the frame on the floor, and bends over to pick it up. "You broke it."

"Change them with what? With the batteries that are under my ass?"

"You watch your mouth," she warns sternly.

"There are no fucking batteries in this house. There never are. Just like there's no toilet paper. Or milk. Or laundry detergent."

"What are you so angry about?" my mom shouts, holding the pieces of the frame in her hand. I don't answer because I hate her standing there with that stupid picture of perfect dead Bradley with his immortal sweet smile. "Seriously, Melissa. What the fuck is wrong with you?"

I open my mouth, but nothing comes out. *Are you kidding me? You have no idea? Haven't you taken a look at our lives?* I'm so stunned at how clueless she is that I don't know what to say. And I can't believe she swore. Can't believe she's angry at *me*.

"What? Tell me," she persists.

"I don't know." I back off, unable to tell her the truth: that I'm pissed she's having a baby. "Everything."

"Like what? Say something. Say one exact thing. One exact thing that you're so goddamn angry about. Come on, I'm waiting ... Something exact."

I so want to tell her. It's on the tip of my tongue, but I know it will make everything worse. "I can't. You can't ask me like that. It's just shit. It's everything. I don't know. This shit, here. All of it. I'm just angry."

"Well, you need to chill," my mom warns, starting to cry. She walks past me and into the kitchen. I don't know what's happening with her and Scott, but she's completely unravelling. "I can't live like this."

"*You* can't? *You* can't live like this? Is every fucking thing about *you*?" I shout behind her, but she turns on the tap and drowns me out.

Part of me feels bad for being so mean to her. A baby isn't the end of the world. And I know my anger is more than just about the baby. It's not her fault that I'm a totally miserable human being. Not entirely, anyway. But the more miserable I am, the more angry I get and the more cruel I am to her.

She doesn't talk to me the rest of the day, which makes me feel totally guilty, as usual. Even though I don't know what for. She's my mom. She's supposed to take my crap. Then, after a bit of time has passed, I try to think more about her question. Why *am* I so mad? And I just don't know. I just am. Always have been.

Thirty-Six

The party on Friday night is at some girl's house. I'm with my friends Ally, Jess, Jasmyn, Liz, and Shayla. I'm ready to get wrecked out of my mind. Around midnight, we are all chillin' in the living room when I decide to go to the kitchen to get some more vodka. When I'm there, minding my own business, this guy's little sister I barely know gets all up in my face like she wants to rush me. She's talking about Fortune being her boyfriend and how I'm a "skank." She's a little taller than me, a little fatter, and has these pathetic cornrows, and I'm sure she thinks she's going to kick my ass. But what she doesn't know is that I feel like killing someone right now and that it takes me zero to ten to lose it, and by the time her adrenalin gets to six, she'll be on the floor. Which is what happens before any of the skank's friends can even cross the room and come to her rescue. It wasn't even that hard. Just a few pushes and she was down.

Before I can do any more damage, Jasmyn and Ally have appeared at my side to shout shit at the girl's friends, who are shouting back. It's all so crazy.

"Let's go," I command, and turn, knowing my girls will

have my back as we go down the hallway and leave through the front door.

It ruins our night. Ally, Shayla, Jasmyn, and I hang out at Coffee Time to sober up, while the others go home. We sit at the table near the back, by the toilet, where the owner lets people smoke late at night. The place is full of scum and drunks and crazies, so we're actually welcomed in comparison. Shayla and Ally both have coffees while I just sit there keeping to myself. They know it takes me some time to come down from fighting and they won't leave me till I'm okay. I sit there half listening to their conversation as I fiddle with my lip, 'cause the bitch somehow got a punch in. I can feel it swelling, and when I suck hard on it I can taste the blood.

"She might charge you," Jasmyn says, who has new-found respect for me now that she's seen me lose it on someone.

I ignore her 'cause I don't feel like talking. Instead, I light a cigarette.

"No she won't," Ally answers for me. "We know her brother. He's got a grow op in their basement. She can't say anything and she knows it."

"I'm not that stupid," I add. It's important you figure this shit out before you throw the first punch, otherwise you'll get charged.

"Actually, the skank's brother will probably beat her more when he finds out it was Mel," Shayla adds, laughing.

"What about her friends?" Jasmyn asks.

"They're nothing," Shayla dismisses. "They won't even bother. They know who Mel's friends are."

I keep my eyes on my burning cigarette during the whole conversation. I don't know why this had to happen tonight. It's the last thing I need. It feels good to be with my girls. We've been friends a long time. It's nice to have people who will always watch your back. Sometimes it's more important than family.

I continue listening to them blah-blahing, but I turn my body to stare out the window. A man walks by and then just stops in front of me and looks in through the window. He's middle-aged. Conservative. White. Wearing beige trousers and a boring sweater. Brown hair. Totally nondescript. At first I think he's staring at me, like he's some pervert, but then he licks the tips of his fingers and pushes his thinning hair back into its contained side part. I realize he doesn't even see me. And for a moment, seeing him seeing his reflection, it's like I am witness to how he truly feels about himself. A totally raw and naked, honest appraisal, something you would never show others. It feels so personal that I'm embarrassed. I almost turn away, but really, I'm too intrigued to pull my gaze.

At first there's hope in his gaze. He touches up his hair, squints his eyes, and bites his lower lip like he's pleased with his face. But then there's this pause, an exhale of air and slight shake of the head, like he's experiencing some kind of despairing defeat. And then he just walks away into the night. And it all strikes me as so sad. 'Cause I get it — that awareness that you just have to deal with what looks you have, and that your attempts at improving them better barely matter in the long run.

But then I think about it more, because it actually runs deeper than being disappointed with his looks. It's like I saw how disappointed he was with himself. How unhappy he was in life. And it's so weird to see someone, a grown man, so vulnerable and raw like that. Normally, he'd just be any boring person walking down a boring street. You would never guess all that pain was on the inside.

And I think that's what Michael and I were all about. It was like he caught me staring into my reflection and he saw what I saw: the real me. My true and honest gaze. Someone slowly falling apart. Like those people in the Renaissance portraits at the art gallery: when you look up close, you can see the hairline cracks breaking their faces apart. Only instead of running scared away from my broken pieces, Michael held my gaze and made me realize that maybe something good was there between the cracks.

⟵→

It's so early when I get home that I watch a movie, because I'm still wound up and won't be able to sleep. My mom and Scott show up at three o'clock in the morning and my mom is pissed drunk, which is totally scary because, little does Scott know, she's pregnant. She's all loud and obnoxious and is bitching at Scott in the kitchen. Apparently everything he is doing is wrong. She lays into him relentlessly: he drinks out of the milk carton, he wears those "gay" jeans, he talks like an idiot. It starts out harmless enough—I'm so used to my mom saying that garbage when she's drunk that I don't really even hear it anymore—but then they start talking about her ex, Dirk, whom they must have seen tonight. I hear something new in Scott's voice. An edge. Something sharp. He starts fighting back. He drills her, asking how she knows Dirk and when she last saw him.

When I go into the kitchen to get some orange juice, they don't even say hi. I walk around them like a ghost. They don't even comment on my swollen lip.

"I don't know … he's … it's not like …" My mom slurs her words. "I don't know … maybe I saw him … at … once … it's not like … shit … Crystal speaks to him … she told … I guess once I saw … but what the hell is it to you? Dumbass … you …"

She's so drunk she can't even curse right. She starts to get up in his face. And you can tell Scott is confused and uncomfortable with it, so he sort of pushes her aside. Not really hard, but because she's so drunk, she ends up completely crashing into the kitchen chair, which pushes into the table, which topples the glass vase that's on it, which comes down, barely missing her head and smashing into pieces beside her.

We both stand there. Silent. Staring at her, a crumpled mess on the floor.

My mom looks up at Scott, absolutely horrified. Like he flung her into all this, intentionally banged her up. As if she's some innocent victim of abuse. But he'd never do that. He's not that kind of man. Then she looks at me. I cross my arms and tower above her, unmoved by her pathetic gaze. Instead of helping her up, or picking up the glass, or yelling at Scott, I walk out of the kitchen. Because I sort of think she deserves it. And I'm kind of glad Scott is here to put her in her place. Because I can't lift her up anymore.

Thirty-Seven

Eric sees my swollen lip the moment I walk into his office, even though I tried to cover it with lip gloss and kept my hair dangling down in front of it. "Whoa. What happened to you?"

"Got in a fight." I throw my backpack and jacket on the floor and plunk down into my chair. I tell him what happened. How it wasn't my fault. How this girl just came up to me and caused shit because she was jealous of Fortune and me.

"How serious are you with Fortune?"

"Not."

"You've been seeing him awhile."

"A few weeks. But not serious."

"How badly did you hurt her?"

"I don't know, I didn't stick around to see. I caused her damage, I'm sure. But nothing permanent."

"And how do you feel about that?"

Please. "Are you asking if I feel bad?"

"I'm just asking how you feel about it."

"Well, I don't feel bad, because she's the one who got up in my face. She asked for it. I don't randomly go and beat up people, you know? And if you get up in someone's face, you better be ready to accept the consequences." I start to get angry, because I don't get why I have to justify myself to him. "Why do you care about her? She rushed me. What, you think she gives a shit about me? She thought she could take me. She was wrong. And if she did kick my ass, she wouldn't feel bad either."

"It's hard for me to accept that there isn't any feeling when you hurt someone. You're not a robot. Is there anything at all that doesn't sit right with you?"

"Well. Maybe if I sat and forced myself and made it come out of me, maybe it would be there. But right now …" I pause and look up into my head as if searching my brain, "… there's nothin'." I shrug my shoulders. "Sorry."

"You don't need to apologize."

"You want me to feel bad. I don't. That's just life sometimes. Girls can be bitches. What am I supposed to do? Let her punch me in the face?"

"Of course not. Let me ask you this, without you jumping to conclusions. This is not the first physical altercation you've had with a girl. In no way do I think you bring on these fights. But I get the feeling that they are often about the same thing: guys. And that's one of the things that will happen if you have many partners who have many partners. Why do you think she wanted to fight you?"

"Because I'm with Fortune."

"And so is she?"

"So she says."

"Is it possible?"

"It's possible."

"Well, Fortune is a lucky guy to have two women fighting over him. So, is it possible that the one you should both be mad at is Fortune? Not each other?"

I think about this a second. Sometimes he makes me feel like an idiot. "Probably."

"So tell me again, why are you not mad at him?"

"I am," I say.

Thirty-Eight

I am mad at Fortune.

Even before I came over to AJ's apartment, I was pissed. And it's like I'm trying to find a reason to fight. I know it's crazy, but everything Fortune does and says lately is just plain wrong. Part of the reason is that girl at the party, but it's also because now that I'm almost sure there's no hope of Michael coming back to me, I can no longer look at Fortune as a distraction. Now it's like he's actually a boyfriend, and that makes all his bad points stand out even more.

I just can't bring myself to be nice. I'm a royal bitch, but instead of calling me on it, he just ignores me and chills with four of his friends, who are all gathered around the television watching a football game. Which makes me smoulder in agitation until I find a big enough spark that I explode.

And there it is.

We're sitting watching the halftime show when Fortune puts a pepperoni on the floor, calls the cat over, and then reaches down to put his cigarette out on its back. With pepperoni in its mouth, the cat screeches in response and takes off.

"What the fuck?" I yell, jumping to my feet, watching the cat scurry away down the hall. "What the fuck was that?"

Fortune looks up at me. "What? What?"

"What did you just do?"

He laughs, realizing now what my freak-out is about. "Relax. We do it all the time. Butt is used to it. AJ's been using Butt as an ashtray for years. That's how he got his name. Butt Out." Everyone starts laughing.

"Holy shit!" I look at him like he's the Devil.

"What?" The smile disappears from his face and suddenly he gets all angry. "Why you looking at me like that? It's a fuckin' cat."

I go to look for the cat, who's hiding somewhere, terrified. I find him in the back bedroom, under the bed. I grab a blanket, shoo him out, and throw it over him before he can get away. Predictably, he freaks out, gets all tangled up, and I wrap him tight so he can't move. Almost immediately, I feel him relax in my arms. "Shhhhh …" I comfort him. "It's okay. It's okay."

I reappear in the hallway, the bundle in my arms.

"Where are you going?" Fortune demands.

"Home."

"You can't take AJ's cat."

"I'm taking him."

"You can't steal someone's fuckin' cat."

"I'm not stealing him. I'm rescuing him."

He laughs, glancing at his friends, who seem to be rather amused by the whole thing—even AJ, who clearly doesn't care about his cat.

"Take the mothafuckin' pussy," Fortune says. "Who the hell cares."

"Exactly. No one cares." I turn and walk away, wondering if he'll yell or come after me. But he doesn't. There's just collective, male, stupid-ass laughter. "You're all fucking morons," I mumble.

I bring the cat home and put him in our washroom. Cats like little places. Having been traumatized, he'll lay low for a few days. I wish Michael were here — he'd know exactly what to do. I leave the blanket on the floor so he can disentangle himself. I get the cat food I bought at the corner store, and a water dish. Then I get the recycling blue box, lay it on its side, and stuff it next to the toilet. He'll need somewhere to hide when we go in there. I put a sign on the door for my mom and Scott.

BEWARE! POST-TRAUMATIC STRESSED CAT INSIDE.
WON'T HURT YOU, BUT DON'T TOUCH.

I go to bed early, feeling totally sorry for myself and my pathetic life. The cat's desperate *meow meow meow* from inside the washroom echoes throughout the apartment. His scratchy, desperate cries make me feel all the sadder and more pathetic. Just when I try to like someone, to get over Michael, I fall for an asshole.

Then the cat's meows get louder and uglier, changing from sad to annoying. I eventually become so pissed off that I have to get up out of bed. "You're an idiot," I scold him when I open the bathroom door and see his scared face peeking out from inside the box. I get down on my knees and reach in, soothing him with my now gentle voice. "It's okay. It's okay. You're safe now—"

Hssss. He lashes out with his paw.

"Owww!" I scream, pulling my hand away, two long streaks of blood already pooling. I punch the top of the container.

"Shithead!" Then I run my hand under cold water, staring at the stinging, swelling skin.

Afterward, I bend back down to look inside. The cat peers out with shiny green eyes. "It's okay ... I know you're just scared."

I head back to my room, my hand now wrapped in toilet paper and carrying the recycling box. I put the box down on the floor beside the bed, figuring the cat will probably go under there at some point during the night.

Little does he realize, I think before I go off to sleep, how similar we are. He's more scared in this safe place than he is in his familiar home of tortured hell. He's so fucked up, he only feels good when he feels bad.

Thirty-Nine

I drag my ass to my regularly scheduled appointment every Monday with Eric. As soon as I go through the door, I'm Echo. There's so much I don't tell him now, about my mom and Fortune and Michael, there's almost no point in seeing him, except that I have to. It's like I'm not even present in the room. I just let Echo blah blah blah ...

But this time I do have a reason for coming. It takes me almost the whole hour to gather the courage to ask. "You know that group home you told me about a long time ago?"

"Yeah," Eric responds.

"I'm not saying I want to go, but I'd see it. Take a tour or something."

"Sure. Any time. All you have to do is call. I have the number here, if you want to do it now."

A panicked feeling rises in my chest, even though I'm the one who brought it up. I've been thinking about moving out for a while now. I don't have money for rent, and since Michael's gone, maybe a group home is my only choice. Still, when it seems like it could actually happen, I start to second-guess myself. Living with ten other messed-up girls?

Having staff around all the time, enforcing rules and giving you "community time" like it's a reward? Having to share a room? "I didn't mean now," I retract. "I can't do it now. Maybe soon."

"Okay. It's just a call, though. Doesn't mean you actually go. You just ask when you can drop by." As he's talking, he opens his book to find the number. "I'll call for you. No pressure at all. Just so you know when their times are."

He dials and talks to someone he knows. Says he has a client interested in checking out the house. He's all casual, like it's no big deal. Then he hangs up the phone and turns to me. "Every Wednesday afternoon, one o'clock. If you want, we can book a personal time." He writes down some stuff on a piece of paper and passes it to me. Before I know it, I have the address and phone number of the group home in my hand.

"Thanks," I say, wondering what the hell I just did.

"No problem. If you want me to go with you, I'm happy to do so."

"Yeah. No. Thanks. I'm just thinking about it. You know?"

He leans forward a little. "You okay, Melissa?"

I lean back, reclaiming the safe gap between us. "Yeah. Yeah. I'm okay. Why?"

"You seem a little … distracted. Tired, maybe? Something happen?"

"Happen?" Echo shrugs her shoulders and pushes farther back into the chair. "Not really. Just thinking about a change."

We sit there and Echo talks about nothing important for a while longer. Meanwhile, the words I really want to say rip up my insides like stabbing knives. *I want to get the fuck out of my house. I want to get the fuck out of my life. I won't let my mom bring me down again. I won't take care of her and a kid.*

I hate everyone — my friends, my mother, Fortune. I even hate Michael. I hate my school. My city. My life. My clothes. My face. Everything. I want out. Out of this head. Out of this body. I want to get the fuck out of this skin.

Forty

I stay in bed for a few days. Sometimes I do this, when things get to be too much. Especially when the weather is crap. When things are grey and ugly and the trees have no leaves and it's like the sky is an inevitable looming overcast of gloom. I feel like my head is a cement block that I'm dragging around. I am numb and there's nothing inside. I don't care about failing school, or pissing off my friends, or hurting my mother. I just don't care.

My mom comes in every morning, yelling and trying to get me to go to school. Ms. Dally calls and threatens discharge from the program if I don't get to class. But none of it matters to me. I just want to sleep all day. I just want to turn off and disappear into a shadow.

On Saturday afternoon, Ally calls me while I'm making Kraft Dinner. I complain about how miserable I am. Every second word is a swear word. She thinks that Fortune and I should get back together because it will make me happier. I tell her, "Not over my dead body."

"So, where's the cat?" she asks, seemingly changing the subject.

"I don't see it ever. It lives under my bed."

"Maybe it's dead."

"No. I leave food out and a litter box in my room, so I know it eats and shits."

"So then call Fortune and tell him to take the cat back. Come on."

"No way. I'm not talking to him." And then I add, "Or any other guy besides Michael."

"Okay, this is getting annoying, Mel. Who do you like, Michael or Fortune, huh? Decide. 'Cause I'm sick of hearing about this shit." Leave it to Ally to tell it like it is. She doesn't have Jessica's patience or tact.

I try to make it as simple as possible. "I love Michael. I like Fortune."

"Earth to Melissa: Michael is gone. So maybe you better love Fortune. Love the one you're with, you know the song?"

"You don't understand."

"I don't understand what? What's there to understand? Yeah, okay, so you and Michael were in love. I get that. But he's left you. We talked about this a billion times. He probably freaked out about how old you are. And so he's gone. Are you going to become a nun?"

"I can't go out with someone who treats a cat like that."

"What are you talking about? You get all freaked out about a cat, but you're fine kicking some girl in the face?"

"That's different. She asked for it. This cat did nothing wrong."

"You're crazy. You know that? Fortune's not a bad guy. If he put a cigarette out on *you*, that would be a different story. But everyone knows Butt. Everyone butts out on Butt."

"Have you?"

"No. Are you insane? Come on," she whines, "make up with him. He's *sooo* cute."

It sounds weird her saying that about him, seems so superficial. As if it's something she thinks I'd like to hear. And I don't know why she's going on like that, since she's not truly into guys anyway. I sigh deeply. "Why are guys such assholes?"

"They're born that way. It's just the way it is. So … will you come out with us tonight?"

I sigh again. It'll mean I have to see Fortune.

"Come on. It's Saturday night."

"Yeah. Okay. Only because I don't want to be around home. But he's kidding himself if he thinks I'll talk to him before he gives me one big fat apology."

⌒→

Turns out Fortune's big fat apology is a fantastic night in bed, and by one A.M. all is good. It's hard to break up with someone when the sex is so great. It's like guys who are good in bed get this immunity card that can be played at any time, only it's an immunity dick.

"How's Butt doing?" he asks as I climb out of his bed to get home before my mom wakes up.

"I've named him Ralph. But don't worry, I'm going to give him back this week. He's miserable living with me. He basically lives under my bed."

"Well, I got something for Ralph." He reaches for his jeans on the floor, and into the pocket. I prepare myself for some stupid-ass joke, but instead he pulls out this half-chewed little rubber mouse with wire whiskers. I smile. "It's not new," he says. "It's from my sister's cat."

I reach over and take it. This is the grey part of people I was talking about, this fuzzy space where you just can't easily dismiss people anymore.

"Look at your smile," he teases, all proud of himself.

I hold my hand up in front of my face to hide it. I don't want to give him the satisfaction of thinking he's a good person. I reach down and punch his firm stomach. "Shut up," I say. Then I take off my clothes and get back into bed.

Forty-One

My mom finds me in the laundry room in the basement of the building on Tuesday night. I'm sitting on the dryer, doing my math homework. I've been hiding down here as much as possible, whenever I have to be at home and she's around. We aren't getting along. She's like a yo-yo. Sometimes she's all needy, and then other times (when she's mad at me) she punishes me by shutting her door and ignoring me and making me feel like she can't stand the sight of me.

"There you are," she says, with that sappy look on her face, all droopy-eyed, sad, and pensive.

I'm trapped.

She sits down on the white plastic chair, pulls one of the laundry baskets toward her, and starts sorting our socks and underwear. She looks like hell—straggly hair, no makeup, purplish bags under her eyes.

"Is it Ricky's?" I ask, doing the math and figuring her stress must be that it's probably not Scott's.

She sighs. "I don't know."

"Giovanni's?"

She laughs. "No. Impossible."

"Why?"

"We used protection."

"Ichhh." I make a face. Somehow, the thought of my mom having anything to do with a condom is disgusting. "They're not a hundred percent, you know."

She glares at me in response. "Since when did you become a sex education teacher?"

"Why don't you have an abortion?" I offer.

"Never." She rejects the idea quickly and lowers her hand to her belly. "Out of the question."

I'm unsure what to say to her next. She sits there all mopey, like she wants me to make things better or say the right thing—but what? "You'll be okay"? "You'll make a great mom"? I look to the door, wishing someone would come to rescue me. Someone older and wiser and optimistic.

I try to think of what my mom would say to me if I told her I was pregnant. I wish I were. I wish I had sliced open my skin and pulled out that birth control capsule five months ago. I wish I had Michael's baby in me right now. Is that what my mom was doing—trying to hold on to someone?

"We'll get through it, Mom," I say to her, but then instantly regret my words. I should have said *You*, not *We*. *You* will get through it. Because if she thinks I'm taking care of some baby, she's got another thing coming. I have my own problems. I start to feel really angry. Like, *Screw you for dumping this crap on me. You're an adult. You should know the answers.*

She takes my supportive comment as an invitation to complain. She says she wakes up every morning feeling like she just wants to crawl back into bed. She says she can't even walk past the fridge without gagging. And she's so tired, she can barely stay awake after noon. Part of me worries that she's drinking even though she promised she would stop and even though I checked all the cupboards and her drawers and there was no sign of anything.

She sighs again. "Oh … I just don't know what to do."

I get up to walk out 'cause I'm so angry and I don't want to have a fight. As I pass her, I say, "I'll get extra hours at the clinic."

"It's okay, Hon. It's my problem. I'll figure something out."

I shake my head and roll my eyes. Whatever. I know these complaints mean she's going to stop working soon. "Well, I'll get some more hours anyway," I say, and walk out.

I have no faith in her working it out. And I won't go to a shelter again. And I won't take care of her like I did after Bradley died and my mom vacated her body for about a year, and returned all patched up from therapy. This time I'm old enough to do something about it. This time I'm not going down with her.

Forty-Two

Up, up, up.

Syphilis keeps straining against his rock. Doomed to the eternal attempt with no reward.

Up, up, up out of bed I get.

It's strange, but the worse my mother's life gets, the more inspired I become about my own. It's one thing to mess up my own life, but I'll be damned if I let my mother screw me up because of her mistakes. "You decide to be happy," Uncle Freestyle tells me. "It's a decision." I'm not entirely sure I agree, but for some bizarre reason I get the notion that maybe all the recent events of my life can be seen as necessary things that are forcing me off a certain road and onto another that (unknowingly) is leading to success. Maybe my mom's pregnancy is just the thing I need to kick me in the butt and get me to move into action.

Sometimes I wonder where these bursts of optimism come from, the ones that get me out of bed the first time my alarm goes off even though experience has told me that there's no point, I'll end up in the same place I started from. But like Ms. Dally says, we make our bed each day knowing that we'll only mess it up again that night. Sometimes the only point to anything is the attempt, because the alternative, never trying, can only lead to inevitable doom.

I start to make plans to move out, get a second job, maybe even have my own apartment. At school, I tell Ms. Dally that I want to make a resumé so I can find work to fill the gaps in between my veterinary clinic shifts. When I say this, it's like I just told her she won a thousand dollars, because she gets all excited and starts putting piles of papers and folders and booklets on my desk, and for a second I regret having said anything because it looks like too much work. But then she guides me toward the computer and we start writing my resumé right away using a special program, and it looks so professional to see my name in bold at the top of the page. After, we write lists of places where I'll drop it off: McDonald's, Coffee Time, Walmart.

I feel so good about everything, for the first time I tell her about wanting to be a veterinarian.

"Fantastic, Melissa. You're certainly off to a good start with your job. And you're great at math," she says in such a teacherish tone that I quickly look over my shoulder to make sure no one is listening. I feel silly that I'm feeling all proud about her dumb comment, like I'm some goody-goody teacher's pet.

All week I work on a career studies project on veterinarians. I spend a lot of time researching on the internet, and I even interview Dr. Keystone at the clinic. My mom buys me a cool Duo-Tang with a clear plastic cover to put the project inside, and when I give it to Ms. Dally she exhales in elation. For the first time in my life, I'm actually proud of something I've done in school.

Forty-Three

Up. Up. Up.

I find the paper Eric gave me, call the group home and make an appointment. The supervisor, Pat, takes me on a tour of a huge old-lady house that feels a hundred years old. Even the furniture smells old and musty. At first, I think it is a mistake to be there and I almost walk out. But then I see a list of names on the fridge and some photos, and it turns out the group home is the same one that Jasmyn and Snow, a pregnant girl who used to go to the day program, are living at.

I stop and point to the photo. "I know these girls."

Pat is immediately at my side. "You do?"

"Yeah, Snow and Jasmyn."

"Ah!" She raises an open hand to stop me from speaking. "You shouldn't have told me any names. We're unable to discuss the whereabouts of our clients. And it doesn't help in your application if you know current residents. It's necessary for us to keep a safe mix of girls here."

Residents? Clients? Safe mix of girls? What is this place?

"Can we wear shoes?" I ask sarcastically.

She smiles, knowing exactly what I'm saying. "It's not prison. You can wear shoes."

Pat's smart. I like that. I like her.

⌒

At the end of the tour, we sit in this teeny room by the front door, crammed with a desk, a computer, and a futon couch. There's barely enough room to stand. I take a seat, squashed up at the desk, and fill out an application. Then Pat gives me a list of house rules to help me decide if it's the right place for me. The list is long. Real long. She tells me if I want to continue with the application, we'd have a few more meetings. "You know, Melissa, you *might* actually enjoy living here. Many girls do."

"Hmmm ... maybe," I respond, wondering if that would be possible. How could I live with so many rules and a bunch of girls knowing each other's business 24−7? Arts and Crafts Night and day trips to Wonderland sound all right, though, as long as the group home pays for everything.

Pat tells me to take a few days to think about it. If I'm interested, I can call her back and she'll set up the last two meetings, one with my mom and one more with just me. Then I can move in right after that. I thank her, take the orientation envelope, and leave.

I decide to walk a few blocks before I hop on the bus. I smoke three cigarettes in a row, trying to work out what's on my mind. Now that the group home might be a reality, I'm feeling kind of scared. It's like committing yourself to jail— you'd have to be insane to do it. But I look at my life and what's happening, and I'm only sixteen. It can only get worse. My mom will never give me rules, and even if she did, I wouldn't follow them. And I can't get my own apartment yet because

I don't have the money. Or if I wanted to save up for first and last month's rent, I'd have to quit my job at the animal hospital to get another one that pays better. I could move in with someone, like Jasmyn's friend, but then I'd only party all the time. And for sure I'd end up dropping out of school. And then what?

I turn onto a side street to take a shortcut. This car speeds past and — SPLAT! — a squirrel appears from beneath the tire. I can't believe it! It's horrifying! A black blob is lying on the road about twenty metres up ahead, and just as I'm about to rush out to see if I can help it, I see this little baby squirrel, all patchy fur and twitchy tail, tentatively move toward the body. It pauses and then approaches slowly to nudge the mother with its little nose. It pokes and nudges and steps back, then climbs right on top of her and nudges more, carefully inspecting. An approaching car scares it away up a tree, but then it comes back again, climbing up on her.

"Ooohhhh!" I shout, and hurry my pace, worried that the baby will get run over too. When I reach the body, the baby runs up the tree again and waits on a low branch, watching me inspect the remains: eyes bulging out, lower body squashed, blood coming out of its bum. Totally dead.

I don't want to touch it, but I don't know how to move it, so I end up pushing it along the ground with my foot to the gutter. I look up to the baby, who is now halfway down the trunk, watching me closely. Poor thing. But what can I do?

I step back and let the baby examine its mother's dead body once more. It nudges and pokes with its nose, climbs on top again, and sort of sits there. Another car whips past, but it doesn't scurry back up the tree 'cause it's safely by the curb now. I watch the baby for about ten minutes before I walk away. It's the saddest thing to see. The baby just doesn't understand what happened to its mother. And it won't leave the useless carcass because it doesn't know what to do without her.

I decide to walk the extra few blocks to the subway station. Mother Nature has a funny way of sending me messages. It's not the first time something coincidental has happened to me like this. It's strange, because just before the squirrel got hit I was starting to think about my mom and having to tell her about the group home, and I was imagining how upset she'd be. Even though I make her life hell, I think deep down she knows she'd be lost without me. I was thinking I'd feel too guilty to leave her alone and then—BAM!—this baby loses its mama but it can't let her go, even when it must in order to survive.

Forty-Four

For some reason I get all clingy with Fortune. I hate losing control and I hate myself for being that way. Even when I'm doing it, I'm aware that I'm being an idiot, but I just can't stop myself. It's like I have this addiction, this yearning in the pit of my stomach that needs its hourly fix. I call him a thousand times a day, I walk by his house hoping to bump into him, I email him and text him. The more I do all this, the less he wants to see me. And even though I know this, I still do it.

My thoughts are crazy. I think he's found someone else. I think he's avoiding me. I think he doesn't like me anymore. One afternoon I wait outside his house till he gets home and then I show up at his door and basically jump him. I give him such amazing sex he's bound to want me more. Then, when he goes to shower, he leaves his jeans on the floor and I get the phone out of the pocket to check his text messages. It's just what I thought: full of messages from girls. *Baby. Honey. Miss you babe. Want you. Kiss* …

When he comes back, I confront him, holding the phone up in the air, reciting the messages. He grabs it out of my hand and starts erasing.

"Don't bother! I've already seen them!"

He whips the phone down onto the bed and then pauses a second, like he's thinking about what to say next. Then he glares directly up at me. "Why are you going through my phone? Why are you in my property?"

And just like that, he turns it around. Instantly, he's the one who gets to be angry. Suddenly I'm on the defence, despite the fact I just caught him fooling around with a ton of girls. "You're an asshole. You know that?" I start to walk away.

"It's nothing, babe. They're just texts. It don't mean nothing."

"I've read them." I raise my pitch to a flighty-girl voice. "*Miss you. Love you. Baby …*"

"They don't mean nothing."

"Who — the girls or the texts?"

"Both." He comes toward me, all sexy with a sweet smile. His shirt is off and his skin is still wet. "Come on, babe, you're the only one. You're the one for me."

"Puh-leeze! You think I'm an idiot?" I push him away and grab the cellphone off the bed. "Get away from me, prick. You can take those girls. All of them. Go fuck them. Go use them. Go party with them … You can have all of them. Know why? 'Cause you don't deserve me." I'm talking fast and crazy and can't stop myself even though I know I should shut up. I keep going, blah blah blahing, clenching the phone in my hand. I head toward the window. "'Cause I'm better than that. I can't believe I fell for a stupid loser like you, driving around in your stupid-ass car like you're all that. And you're nothing. You're a piece of shit. You're a fucking dumb-ass —"

"Shut up!" he shouts forcefully. He reaches out to grab my arm as I'm about to chuck the phone at the window. He squeezes so tight I drop to my knees in response. He holds my arm up above my head and I feel like it will rip out of its socket. "Let go," he warns in a growly voice. I drop the phone. He releases his grip, leaving my skin burning. I quickly stand up, but then he pushes me. "Bitch!"

He pushes so hard I go flying and hit the corner of the dresser and then fall to the ground. My ribs pain. I lose my breath.

It's like everything is still for a minute.

I don't breathe.

I don't blink.

My face is flat against the hardwood floor.

My lips hang loose from my face, my mouth open wide.

I look out of the corner of my eye and see his expressionless face towering above. He doesn't move to help me. And for a split second it's like I have become my mother. That night she fought with Scott. And it's like I'm in her skin. And I see myself and her all at the same time, like we're this overlapped person in the same body. And then … "Huuuhhhh." I take a choky, choppy gasp.

Breathe.

I scramble to my knees, onto all fours, and then up. I grab my backpack and coat and rush toward the door because I'm afraid of what might happen next.

As I run down the stairs, trying to put my jacket on, his voice trails after me. "What about you? All the guys you fuck? Everyone knows you're a slut! You know what they call you? Black hole. You bitch. Yeah! You hear me? 'Cause guys disappear inside your huge, slutty pussy."

His words are like forceful blows as I pass through the front door. I run down the porch stairs, but it seems as if my feet are barely moving. I stop a second to catch my breath.

Everything before me is in slow motion. I take it in all at once, like a painting. A sharp, cold wind blows the single remaining yellow leaf off a tree. Threatening black clouds surge. A woman walks her little white mutt past the driveway. A red car goes by. A squirrel prances across the road then up onto the fence that separates Fortune's house from his neighbour's.

A bang from inside the house brings me back to reality. I begin to move again. Another gust of wind takes my hair and blows it up and all over my face, into my mouth, but I don't stop to take it out. My legs just go. Too scared to think. Just running against the strong wind. Fight or flight. I choose to fly.

⟶

I start bawling again when I get into my room. I take off my top to inspect my ribs. Already my skin is red and purple from hitting the furniture. Slut? After being with me, after saying he loved me even though we both knew it wasn't true, he calls me slut? Uncle Freestyle was right, guys do talk shit about you. Not that I really care. Jerk. I hate Fortune. I fucking hate him. I knew he was with other girls. I hate all men.

I go into the kitchen and down three shots of vodka and wait for my head to clear. I turn on the TV and flick the channels. Then I go take three more shots.

Even when I start feeling drunk, I still feel a little weird. Shaky. Like I'm scared or something. I hate myself for being afraid of him. It's stupid. It's not like anyone has ever hit me before. I've seen it happen to my mom, when I was little and she had some idiot boyfriends. So maybe that's why I expect it will happen to me. When a guy raises his hand, I brace.

I hate this weakness. I hate being a girl. There's always this inevitable submission. Men will *always* have the last word. The last fist. They will always have that ultimate power.

⟜

Sometimes, when I'm feeling really bad, I reach into my mind and bring out a memory of Bradley. It's the only thing that can possibly make me feel better, as if somehow I'm not alone. As if somehow the ghostly memories bring his spirit to my present. I go take two more shots and lie back down on the couch, just letting my mind roam, like one of those roulette machines that bounces a ball around until it randomly lands on a number. My head spins and spins and spins until it lands on this:

I'm playing with Bradley on the front lawn of our apartment building. His favourite thing to do was spin. I'd take his wrists and pull him up into the air and twirl around and around, his feet flinging wildly. I have this image of his face imprinted on my mind: his open, laughing mouth, his ecstatic eyes locked on mine, intoxicated with his cocktail of pleasure and thrill and trust all mixed together. I remember loving this face 'cause I could recall feeling like that when I was younger. I used to cherish that feeling of weightlessness.

"Faster!" he'd shout tirelessly. "Faster!" And I'd propel his featherweight body through space till my arms ached and I had to let him drop. And his bare legs dragged along the ground, leaving him with green grass-stained reminders of the inevitable fall, because everyone, even little kids, must pay some kind of price for the dizzy high.

Suddenly my stomach churns. I jump up and run to the toilet, grip it with both hands, and hurl into the brown-stained bowl. Just the stench of the toilet bowl makes me puke more. When I'm done, I lower myself onto the bathroom tiles and curl up in a ball, lying on my side. It's dark. I didn't turn on the light. I hear my breathing. And a slight pounding in my head.

My mind spirals down to somewhere dark and cold. I suppose it's natural to think only of the good times with Michael, but the bad memories have always been there, hovering somewhere in the past. Sometimes, it's the body that remembers. Sometimes, the body's memory is so much more powerful than the mind's. Even if you don't want to think about it, even if you fight it, the moment comes to you anyway in its entirety, flashing through your mind, smashing your skull like a bullet.

It happened on our last night. Before he said the words and I walked out the door.

Michael had applied for teacher's college before I met him. He was so nervous about it, always saying he feared he wouldn't get in. I knew it would be no problem because his high school marks were so good, even if he did drop out of his science degree. But he said the acceptance would depend on a number of things, like volunteer work and experience, so it was all a gamble. He was all doomsday-like, which made me oddly optimistic. I swear, if you want to cure depression, put a sad person around someone even sadder, and that's better than five years of Prozac.

The closer the acceptance deadline came, the more agitated he grew. And when the acceptance deadline passed, it was like there was an instant fog over his eyes.

"You'd make a great teacher," I encouraged. I was jumping up and down on his bed while he sat at his desk surfing the Web. "Maybe you could teach at my school. Excuse me, Mr. Butler?" I raised my hand as I jumped. "Excuse me, Mr. Butler, but may I go to the bathroom? And Mr. Butler, while I'm in the bathroom, can we have sex?"

Michael threw a pillow at me. "Stop it. That's gross. I couldn't be your teacher. That would make me some kind of pervert."

"So what are you now?"

He turned in his chair and stared strangely at me. "I don't know. Not a pervert. Maybe fucked up. Maybe irresponsible. But not a pervert."

"Pervert. Pervert. Pervert …" I taunted, turning round and round on the bed, bouncing up and down.

Oomph.

My feet were pulled out from beneath me and I landed face first on the bed, just inches away from the wooden headboard. I was stunned, the air knocked out of me. Michael was on my back, pinning me down, knee digging into my spine. Despite the soft mattress, I felt like I was being crushed. I felt his hot breath at my ear. I held my own breath. I closed my eyes. I braced.

"It's not a joke," he said firmly, in a gruff, deep voice. An old voice. A voice that sounded twenty-eight.

Forty-Five

I'm fired.

Dr. Williams asks me to come into his office as soon as I arrive at work. He gets all serious and tells me someone has tampered with the filing cabinet in his office. He says he has a security camera and knows that it was me.

"Where's the camera?" I ask, sensing that he's lying. Adults who don't have a lot of experience with teenagers are so transparent. They think we're six-year-old gullible kids who will believe anything.

"It's hidden," he says. Then he swallows. A sure sign of lying.

"So what did you see?" I challenge him, because he'd have to mention Rachel being in the room if there was really a camera. "If you saw me, who else did you see? Was anything taken?"

"You know what happened, Melissa."

"No, I don't." I start to get angry. "What happened? Tell me. Exactly. What did you see?"

"Melissa, I don't think there's any point arguing about it. I've met with the team and we've made our decision. We are such a small office and we need to trust our employees. There are valuable things in this clinic that we could be really liable for if they were to get into the wrong hands."

I know what he's saying. He's talking about the painkillers. I shake my head at the injustice of it all, that I'm immediately typecast as a punk 'cause I'm the poor girl, not like Rachel. So what if I broke into the cabinet? Who am I hurting? "I only took a phone number. I didn't take anything important," I finally admit.

He shrugs his shoulders, all sorry-like, as if it's too late for him to change his mind.

It gets all awkward and I don't know what to say. And he just stands there, like he's waiting for me to leave. But I've been here for almost two years. And I'm great at my job. And I love the animals. And I worked so hard. And I didn't steal anything but a stupid number. And I can't imagine my life without this place. And it's my only connection to Michael ... "But I love this job," I plead. I feel like I'm about to cry.

"I'm sorry, Melissa. You really did well here. We just can't ... Our team already met ... I tried ... It's a shame. I'm really upset it happened. I know it's hard for you and your mom ... I just wish ..."

My mom? Where did that come from? What does he know about my mom? "It's okay," I say, quickly turning to walk out the door because I don't want him to get all pitying over me. I rush down the hallway, wiping my face with my shirt. I feel like I should take something, do something, tidy up something ... but there is nothing of mine here. Not even a left-behind jacket or a notebook. Nothing.

I don't want to see anyone, so I leave by the back door. And that's where I see Rachel, wearing a matching red ski jacket and wool hat, walking a stupid beagle across the parking lot. Then it occurs to me: it was Rachel who ratted. It had to be. My sadness immediately turns to anger.

"Why did you tell them?" I demand, approaching her.

"I didn't. Tell them what?"

"About the file cabinet."

She walks past me, hurrying her pace. Dragging the dog a little. "They asked me."

"So lie!" I follow her, trailing her closely through the parking lot.

"I can't."

"Why not?"

"Because it's wrong."

What? What a stupid thing to say. "Because it's wrong?" I say, mocking her. "Who the fuck cares if it's wrong? What business is it of yours?"

She turns a little to walk around her princess-white Mini, parked just by the back door. "It's wrong," she repeats with growing confidence now that the car is between us. "And if I see wrong, it's my responsibility to do something about it. That's the problem with society—people just turn a blind eye."

I screw my face up in disgust. "Are you for fucking real?" It's as if she was spoon-fed the words during a little dinnertime talk with her family. "What language are you speaking? I see your lips moving, but it's like an old lady talking."

"Don't get mad at *me*, Melissa. You're the one who did it. You stole something."

"God, Rachel," I say, exasperated. "Life's not so fucking simple."

She crosses her arms and stands firm. "Mine is," she says, smirking.

And that stabs me more deeply than any knife could do. Rachel is no innocent uptown girl—she knew the precision of her words. Instantly, it's like this huge divide opens between us. Like some earthquake crack parts us. And I hate her. I hate her life. I hate her fucking car. I hate her stupid, prissy face. I want to kill her.

I look around, then down, searching for something. I don't know … something. Anything. Then I see it: a big piece of wood sticking out of the metal garbage bin behind me. I pick it up, hold it high above my head like I'm going to launch it at her. I won't, but I want to scare her. She ducks, and then I bring it down hard onto her car windshield. It smashes. A muffled crunch. A punctured round centre, with cracks snaking out from it.

She gasps. So do I. I can't believe I did it. My hands throb. She looks up, horrified, then terrified that I'll come after her. She drops the dog's leash and it starts to hobble away, back toward the patch of grass.

She starts crying and her face gets red. "You're fucking dead! You're fucking going to jail!" she shouts as she runs around the side of the building, down the driveway, and toward the front door of the clinic.

"Shit! Shit! Shit!" I look around for a second, trying to take in what just happened. "Fuck!" I hurl the wood into the bin and then quickly run after the stupid dog, which is wobbling toward the road. I drag it back, its reluctant little nails scraping along the pavement, and loop its leash around the car antenna.

Then I take off.

Forty-Six

I always fuck up.

Before I get out of the boat, I must get *in* the boat.

I'm not even *in* the goddamn fucking boat yet.

I stand barefoot in the sooty mud by the riverbank. The tall reeds brush against my face as I reach out to the edge. I hold up my frilly dress in one hand while still managing to lift myself in. The water splashes, echoing in my head. Beautiful. I take the oar and push it into the soft ground, propelling the boat off the bank. And then I'm taken by the current. I lie down on the wooden seat, at first staring into the rippling water, then staring at the blue, blue sky. I close my eyes. Still drifting, drifting, drifting. Then I slip one foot over the edge.

I can't sleep.

How many days since I bashed in the car? Five now?

I can't sleep.

Each night, I wait for the police to come to my door. Listen for the knock. Wait for my mother's devastated face. Wait for them to take me away in the back seat of the cruiser so I can spend the night in some shitty dorm room with some screwed-up girls who scare the hell out of me and make me seem like a princess.

In the middle of the night, I hear my mom in the living room. I guess she can't sleep either. I don't go see what she's doing, but I know she's upset because Scott has left her. She finally told him about the pregnancy, hoping he would assume it was his, but it turns out he got snipped a few years ago. They had a huge fight and somehow she turned it all around and got mad at him for lying all this time about the vasectomy. He said he never told her because he didn't think it mattered because she had said she was done having kids.

That was only a couple of days ago, but since then she's seemed really out of it. Which gives me a panicked feeling, because I just don't trust her. I look at the clock: three A.M. I close my eyes to try to go back to sleep, but my mind races ... She'll start drinking ... Her kid will be born a retard ... She's probably long gone off her medication ... We are going to lose the apartment ... I can never move into the group home now, because if I do, my mom won't get her child benefit government money for me, and if she doesn't get that, and she's not working, she'll lose the apartment ... But we'll probably lose it anyway, and then we'll be homeless ... CAS will probably leave me alone because I'm sixteen, but they'll take my mom's baby ... especially if we're homeless ... especially if I'm in jail. Which is where I'm going now. Jail. Because of that stupid bitch Rachel.

Forty-Seven

Everything has changed. Now that I don't have my job, I don't have a future. How can I be a veterinarian if I get fired from my first job in a veterinary clinic? How can I get into university without that reference? I was such an idiot to even think it was possible.

It's like all that learning has been for nothing, because I'll never get the life I want. Something is always going to drag me down. What's the point of even trying? So every day before school, I meet up with Tyler in the park and we drink, because I still have to go to school and it's the only way to make it bearable. I usually miss the first period. When I finally get to the church, I brush my teeth in the washroom and chew tons of grape bubblegum. No one notices, because I'm not drunk out of my mind, just enough to get my work done. Just enough to shut off all that misery for a while.

But today, right in the middle of class, Ms. Dally tells me to go into the couch room. Without asking why, or making a scene, I just do what she tells me. I sit in the corner of the green paisley couch, waiting, reviewing today's list of misdemeanours. Does she know I smoked before school? Does she know I cheated on my math test? Does she know there's a half-empty bottle of vodka in my bag?

"You're not in trouble," she assures me as she walks in. She closes the door behind her and comes to sit on the couch beside me. She smiles warmly. "I just wanted to talk to you. Are you okay?"

"Yeah." I wriggle uncomfortably in my seat. It's going to be one of *those* conversations.

"I'm asking because you seem upset."

"I'm fine." I'm being a bitch to her and I know it, but I don't really care.

"Well, I'm in the classroom trying to teach you math, but to be honest, it feels a little awkward because you seem so distant. You're really resisting. And I feel that perhaps algebra is rather unimportant in comparison to what you might be dealing with. I just don't want to push you too much, Melissa. I want you to know you could draw in your sketchbook or journal for a while if you'd like."

"I'm okay," I insist.

She sighs. It's not the right answer and she keeps looking at me with these sympathy eyes like she's trying to coax the tears out of me.

"Can I be honest, Melissa?"

Leave me alone! I shrug my shoulders. "Whatever."

"You look like you're going to crack. Break open. Like you're on the edge and you're barely holding it together."

It's a terrible thing to say to someone. It's like telling someone they look tired. Who wants to hear how shitty they look? Who wants to hear that they look like a miserable, unstable wreck? "I'm okay," I repeat, annoyed. "I mean, I'm not happy, but I'm not gonna start bawling or throwing up or having a seizure or something, if that's what you mean."

She keeps looking at me and I feel horribly transparent

now. It's as if she wants her analysis of me to come true. She wants me to break open right here and spill myself onto the floor. "Is anything on your mind you want to talk about? Is there stuff going on at home?"

"At home? No," Echo says.

Silence.

I can't bear the quiet. I have an urge to fill it. "There is always stuff going on at home," I add.

"Do you want to talk about it?"

"No."

"What about the group home? Sheila told me they called a few days ago to set up your last intake appointment with your mom. She left a message at your house."

I raise a brow and look at her. My mom has never mentioned anything to me. "Really?" I had forgotten about the group home. I can't believe I actually was considering it. I shrug my shoulders. "I changed my mind. I don't want to go anymore."

Ms. Dally sighs. "That's too bad, Melissa. I think it would have given you and your mom a break. Allowed you some breathing space to get things on track. Okay ... Well. They say you're a good candidate and you can reapply any time. In the meantime, do you have someone to talk to about what's happening in your life?"

"Yeah."

"Who?"

"My friends. My uncle."

"Good. Well, if you need to talk, I'm here. And in the meantime, if you need to journal or to take a break from school work and sketch, then tell me."

"Okay."

Her intentions are good, but I've met countless optimistic, fresh-faced adults who think they can help me. Like they're going to be the one who makes me cry or remember or confess or release or forgive. But there comes a point when you've just talked enough and you realize that talking can't ever help you. You talk to counsellors and uncles and friends and boyfriends, and all that conversation—all those suggestions and interpretations—doesn't change a thing. When their mouths finally shut, you still have the same family. The same life. The same sadness. The same fog in your head that dulls everything.

I ask to go to the washroom, where I look at my face in the mirror. I *do* look terrible. I have zits all around my mouth and forehead. My hair is greasy and tangled. My roots are black. My eyes are puffy. My eyeliner is running.

I put on some shiny pink lip gloss and try to puff up my hair. Then I move in closer toward my reflection and consider the person who is looking back at me. Maybe my eyes do look sad, but I don't think I look like I'm going to break. One thing about feeling shitty inside is that you think you're doing a good job of covering it up. So that no one will ask. So that no one will speculate.

You look like you're going to crack. Ms. Dally's words echo in my head. I pull back and give myself the finger and simultaneously stick my tongue out. "Fuck you," I say to my reflection, and then I put my baseball cap on and pull it down to hide the hairline cracks that are spreading across my face.

Forty-Eight

I feel so empty. Everything inside is dry and brittle, and I just don't care what happens to me or anyone else. I almost forgot this emptiness when I was with Michael. But it's back now, more hollow than before. When you're living in this void, the only thing to do is party and get high. So that Nathan's hand slipping into my underwear can turn me on even though I wouldn't look twice at him if I were sober. Even though it's the K that's making me so horny I want to screw his brains out. On K, it's like all I want to do is have sex. And the more I have sex, the more stuff Nathan will give me to stay high.

So we go into the bedroom while Ally and Jasmyn and the other guys are partying in the living room. And Nathan and I do it. And I don't care that my boobs are uneven and that my nipples aren't the right size and that my stomach bulges a little. And I don't care about the noises coming out of my mouth. I don't even care that Anthony has opened the door and is standing there, watching. And I don't care that Nathan has an ugly, pockmarked face and a scrawny body and crooked teeth. Because now, him fucking me ... it's as if he's filling me back up with some kind of love.

I don't go home for three nights. I figure this out only when I see my neighbour's newspaper and it says Tuesday. I had lost track of days and nights. The next morning, I feel like hell. I'm sick at home for four days solid. Is that what seventy-two hours of partying will do to you? I throw up all over my bedspread. I have a fever of about 3006. I am too sick even to watch TV— the light pains my eyes. So I lie in the dark, drifting in and out of sleep.

My mom, who looks like more of a wreck than me, doesn't ask questions. I just tell her I have the flu and she brings me chicken soup from a package, and fizz-less Sprite, lays it on the floor on a tray. I tell her if I die, I'd like my body cremated and flung off the Eiffel Tower.

"That would be expensive to fly there," she jokes. "How about the CN Tower?"

"Don't make me laugh," I groan. "It hurts my skin."

Even when I feel better, I don't want to get out of bed, so I fake being sick for two more days. I don't want to go to school. Or eat. Or bullshit smile at bullshit people. I don't want to get high. I don't want to fuck. I don't want to meet Ally after school. I don't want to wear my ugly clothes or brush my ugly hair or look at my ugly face in the mirror.

Forty-Nine

I feel like I'm slipping away from my body. I can barely eat. I just want to fade away. My mom stops talking to me again. Ally and Jess are mad at me because I don't return their phone calls. Fortune is long, long gone, probably moved on to screwing some other stupid girl who believes his lies.

I almost wish the police had come to take me away. I figure Rachel is having some family meetings to plan my capture, so I just have to be patient. Besides, I have more important things to worry about. Since Scott is gone and my mom stopped working and I got fired, there is no money to pay the rent. Even Freestyle has conveniently disappeared, the way he always does when my mom is in trouble. And since we no longer get a break from Giovanni, I'm sure we're soon going to be evicted. I see the unopened bills on the kitchen table. I hear my mom crying on the phone to Crystal. We don't even have one single Christmas decoration up in the apartment.

For some sick reason, I keep threatening my mom that I'm going to move into a group home. It's cruel, I know. I don't know why I do it. I get some cruel satisfaction out of seeing her squirm, even when she's already down and out. It's hard to admit, but I like having that power over her. In retaliation, she's stopped talking to me, like she's trying to give me a taste of what it's like to not have her in my life anymore.

I keep asking her to make up with Giovanni, but it's hopeless. She believes Scott will come back and pay for everything, and she doesn't want to be screwing Giovanni when he does. But I know better. We need Giovanni. I find him in the underground garage, cleaning the air vents. He looks better than he used to. I think he's lost weight. I sit on an overturned garbage bin and make small talk. Then I tell him that my mom misses him, that he should stop by.

"Don't tell me shit," he says. But I know he's hurt, because I can see it in his eyes. She broke his heart, I'm sure. But he won't ever admit it because of his male pride. It's all so stupid. And we are going to end up in a shelter because of it. Someone needs to be the adult in all of this.

Fifty

I'm in the boat now, drifting down the river, staring at the blue, blue sky. I imagine myself floating like one of the white lilies that brush against the bow with a constant shooosh shoosh *sound. I lean to the side and slip one foot up over the edge, bringing the boat's rim close to the water. My stillness steadies the rocking, rocking. I stare into the murkiness. I long to disappear into the deep, deep dark, but the rippling reflection of the golden willows wavering in the breeze pulls my gaze back from the black depth. Then I see the reflection of my own face.*

"Get out of the boat," my reflection says.

But I can't.

I'm caught between the fear of what lies beyond that dark depth and the lure of the beauty mirrored in it. Will I sink or swim? Reflect or get absorbed by the darkness? It's a fifty-fifty chance.

All I know for sure is that if I stay in the boat, there is a certainty of death.

Long blades of grass. Orange, black, brown, green. Grass. Jungle. Trekking. Marching through the hallway-carpet-fibre jungle. I'm a tiger. Rooaarrrr. Ha! Stop. Giovanni's office door. My finger to the plastic sign. Trace the letters, *Su-per-in-ten-dent*. My head spins, spins, spins. So fucking high. How many E's? How many shots? I hold on to the door frame for balance. Disgusting office. Wood panelling. Metal desk. Small, barred windows. Giovanni. His back. His balding head. Tools. Stink. Stink. Oil. Paint. Spread-eagle Miss July humping a red Corvette. Giovanni. Plumber's ass. Gross.

Open my mouth. "Hi." My word hangs in the air in front of me like a cartoon bubble. I reach out to pop it and then laugh.

"Melissa?" He swivels around in the old office chair to face me. The *squeak squeak squeak* pains my ears. My heart is racing.

"I want to do something for you."

"What?"

Get out of the boat. Get out of the boat.

I said, "I wanna fuck."

"Jesus! Are you crazy?" Disgusted face. "Why are you here?"

Get out of the boat.

I shut the door behind me. Trip toward him, swaying my hips all sexy-like. All men are the same. All men are weak. I reach out to put my hand on his belt buckle.

Giovanni's hands go up. "Hey! What are you doing, Melissa? Stop it. Stop." But he doesn't get up. Something in his voice makes me keep going. All men are weak.

Get out of the boat.

"It's okay, I'm old enough," I assure him. I feel powerful. I know exactly what to do. I am forceful. Like he's my bitch. He'll do what I want. "Don't move," I command.

I smell the stink of cigarettes. I smell his dirty hair, his greasy scalp. It makes me gag, but I cover it up with a cough.

I do everything really, really fast so that he can't stop me. I take off my jeans, roll up my top, and stand there in my pink thong underwear and my mom's black lace push-up bra. I take his thick, callused fingers and put them on my stomach. Feels strange. Rough. I slip his hand into my underwear. He pulls it out. "Stop," he says, breathless. I put my hand on his crotch. That's all I have to do. He does the rest. We don't kiss. We don't talk. He doesn't even take off his underwear, just opens his fly. I'm still sitting spread-legged on his lap. And I think we're about to fuck.

"No. No. No," he repeats. At the same time, he takes my hand and it touches his dick and I realize he wants a hand job. So I have to do it, but only for a few seconds before he pushes my hand away and tells me to get out.

I don't know why, but I listen to him. I get off. I put on my clothes. And I walk out of the office.

On the way back up to the apartment, I feel totally great. Like I've taken care of things, even if he didn't cum. I feel like I'm not someone who's going to let life dump its shit all over me. I start laughing down the hallway, really loud. In the stairwell I feel so light I'm flying up the steps. I begin to shout. My shrill voice echoes off piss-stained walls.

"Fuck you, Mom!"

"Fuck you, Michael!"

"Fuck you, Fortune!"

"Fuck you, Rachel!"

"Fuck you, Giovanni!"

⌒

But then later, when the E is dying down, and I'm in the bath with the lights off and I think of Giovanni and his stink and his nasty old-man dick, I start to cry. I cry and cry and cry till my face, my jaw, and my throat hurt. I'm so disgusted, I put the soap in my mouth and on my tongue and rub it on my teeth. I jam the bar under my fingernails and scrub. I put it in my ears, my nose, everywhere, just to get all of him off me. Then I immerse my body in the water, pull my face under, trying to keep all of me, all my skin, submerged. I try so hard to keep myself under the water, but I keep floating. No matter how hard I try to stay sunk, I float.

Fifty-One

When I open my eyes, there are white curtains closing in around me. Am I in a casket? I think it's a dream. A good one: I'm dead. I close my eyes once more, for a few seconds. Then I open them again.

I'm in a hospital bed.

It's noisy.

People shouting. Crazy people shouting.

Beeping.

Loudspeaker.

Pain.

I lift up off the bed. My stomach cramps. Throat raw. Jaw tightens. Nose stings. Dry mouth. *Icch*. What's that taste? I run my hand along my tongue, and then look at my fingers. They have black on them. Black? Oh my God, I'm dying! I turn my head to the side and throw up. A pink plastic bowl appears under my face.

"You're okay, Mel. Just let it happen." My mother's voice is faint, like she's far, far away, only I can smell her breath and I see her hand holding the bowl. "The black is from the charcoal. It's cleaning your system. You had a tube up your nose to aspirate."

The memory of last night starts to come back to me. Me in the bathtub. Then Ally calling some time after that. Her coming to my apartment to get me. Then us going to a party. And the coke. The K. The pills. My head pounds. "Where's Ally?" I manage to scrape the words up my throat.

"She's at home. She brought you in. She's a good friend. I'll call and say you're awake now."

Yes, it's all coming back to me ... Giovanni. The party. The coke. The bathroom floor tiles.

Hospital? Fuck Allison for overreacting and bringing me here—and now for all the shit I'm going to be in. I lift my body a little and squint my eyes, catching my reflection in the metal paper towel dispenser beside my bed. I see my distorted face, my crazy hair, and my black-stained clown mouth. I flop back down. "I wanna go," I croak.

"You will. The psychiatrist needs to see you first."

I close my eyes. "Why?"

"To make sure you're okay. That's all. They have to do it."

"When?"

"Soon."

"What do they want?"

"I don't know," she answers.

But it's obvious. This has happened to people I know before. They want to know if I tried to kill myself. Did I? I'm not even sure. I don't remember. But if I had to guess, if I had to tell the truth, I'd probably say yes. Not really that I tried to kill myself, more that if I had died last night, I wouldn't have cared.

And then it's like all that energy that just woke me up has emptied, and I'm suddenly exhausted and can barely keep from falling asleep. My mother, on the other hand, seems to have been waiting for hours for me to wake up just so she can give me shit.

"What did you take last night, Melissa?"

I roll over onto my side away from her.

"It's bad timing, but Rachel's parents called me yesterday. She's not pressing charges." I start to drift back to sleep. "Her mother called me. You're lucky …"

I ignore her.

"Of course, you'll have to pay for the car."

I don't answer.

"What did you take from work?"

Ughh … Let me not wake up again.

⌒

I pass in and out of sleep for what feels like days. I hear patients around me mumbling and shouting and yelping and groaning. I don't even know if it's day or night; there are no windows and the lights stay on all the time. But it doesn't matter really, because I'm so exhausted all I do is sleep. Then, when I sneak open an eye, I see my mother on the chair drinking coffee, and I know it's morning.

"Good morning," she says cheerfully.

Is it a day later? I try to curl my lips into a smile. I feel them crack.

"How are you feeling?" she asks.

How am I feeling? I am feeling nothing. After throwing up for so long, all feeling has erupted out of me. I think it came out of my mouth—all those black thoughts of death and anger and Michael and Mom. And now I just sort of feel empty. I'm achy and sore and just … broken.

I shrug a shoulder in response, unsure if she sees it or not from under the sheet.

"Well, just rest. And let me know if you want anything."

Before I have a chance to speak, the curtain opens and a woman appears at the base of my bed. She's tall and really pretty: blond hair, perfect bone structure, deep blue eyes.

"Hello, Melissa, Ms. Sullivan," she says in a professional tone, and reaches a hand out to greet my mother. "I'm Claire Macbeth. I'm the social worker in charge of your case. I'm here to answer any questions and to begin a safety plan for you, Melissa."

"Thanks," my mom replies.

"I'm sure you're wondering what's happening here. Let me tell you about our procedure. Melissa, you were told this when you first came in, but you probably don't remember. You've been admitted to the emergency department due to a drug overdose. You were barely conscious and had a weak heartbeat when you were brought in by your friend. We gave you a nasal tube and activated charcoal to aspirate the contents of your stomach. A potentially life-threatening combination of drugs were screened in your system, which quite possibly could have led to cardiac arrest had you not been admitted." As she speaks, her beauty changes to ice and her blue eyes fade to a colourless grey. I turn and look away. Too many words. "You might be angry at your friend now, but it's possible she saved your life," she continues. "We gave you some medicine, so you'll be feeling quite groggy for a while. We also did an internal exam and took some blood to check for anything of concern. In terms of demission procedure, first a child and youth counsellor will come and ask you some questions. And then the psychiatrist will make her assessment."

"So, not much longer, then?" my mom asks. I look back at the woman to hear her answer.

"That's correct," she says in a clipped voice. She backs her way out through the curtain. "Hang in there, Melissa." And then she's gone.

At least a few hours later, the curtain opens again and a spiky-blond-haired guy in his mid-twenties appears at the base of my bed. I quickly close my eyes to pretend I'm asleep. "Hi, Melissa, Ms. Sullivan. I'm Warren, a CYC— that's child and youth counsellor—here at the hospital. I'm here to ask Melissa a few questions. But first, before I begin, do either one of you have any questions for me? I know you've been in here a long time, and it's not the most calming environment."

I don't move.

"We've been in emergency for too long. It's too noisy. How much longer?" I hear annoyance in my mom's voice.

"I apologize, Ms. Sullivan. We're just waiting for the psychiatrist to make her assessment."

"So, not much longer, then?"

"Hopefully not. It'll depend on her assessment. When I go back upstairs, I'll check in on her again to make sure she's on her way."

"Okay. Then I'll leave you two alone," my mom says, and I feel a squeeze on my foot below the sheet. "Do you want anything, Hon?"

I keep my eyes shut.

"No? Okay, then. I'll be back later."

"Hi, Melissa. Can I sit on the edge of your bed?" Warren asks, like he knows I'm faking sleeping.

I raise a hand and gesture "whatever," then I feel the mattress dip.

"I know you're not feeling great now, Melissa. I know the medicine we gave you makes you feel strange, and you don't feel like talking about anything. But to be honest, the sooner we get through these questions, the sooner you can get out of this place. So I'm going to ask you to sit up and give me just fifteen minutes of your time. Then you can go back to sleep again. I promise."

I wait a bit, half considering his proposal and half trying to muster the strength to lift up my throbbing head.

"Can you sit up, please?" he asks, a little more firmly.

I lift my head and push my way up to a sitting position.

"Thanks," he says when I finally reposition myself and stare out at him from empty eyes. "Now, I'm going to ask you lots of things. Some questions will seem strange and others will feel really personal. Try your best to answer as many as you can. What you say is confidential, so your mom won't know. The information is for the psychiatrist's assessment."

He starts right away, asking me tons of questions and writing down my answers. Who do you live with? Do you share a room? Do you have access to a gun? Do you have friends? Have you had sex? What are your grades like? Have you ever tried to kill yourself? Have you ever thought about it? Have you ever been pregnant? Do you take drugs? Marijuana? Cocaine? Heroin? Sedatives? Glue? Can you sleep at night? Do you have an appetite? Would you care if you died? Who would care if you died? Do you know why you are here? What do you want to do after high school?

It goes on forever, but this doesn't seem to bother me. I just answer the questions, one after the other. I tell him the truth. I don't care what he knows. And I tell him everything except for what happened with Giovanni.

"This last one is my favourite," Warren says, finally putting down his clipboard. "If you could make three wishes, what would they be?"

"I don't make wishes."

"If you had to."

"Okay. Off the top of my head? I wish I could go home. I

wish for twenty million dollars. And …" I look at him. "I wish
you'd go away?"

Warren taps his pen against the page and closes the binder.
"Got it," he says, winking. "I'm done. Thanks for hanging in
there."

Warren returns a while later and introduces me to the
psychiatrist. She's a middle-aged, nerdy lady with a whispery,
soft voice. She explains to me that she's just here to talk about
what happened and assess my current state of well-being. She
gives me a fresh hospital gown to put on and then I have to
follow her down the hallway and into this little room with two
chairs and a desk and a window looking into the nurses' station.
She asks me lots of the same questions as Warren, only she goes
more into my mom and Bradley and my counselling with Eric.
Somehow, she even gets me to tell her about Michael, which
at this point I don't care about keeping a secret anymore. I just
want him over with. I want him out of my mind.

By the kinds of questions she keeps asking me, I can tell she
thinks I tried to kill myself. Then finally she comes right out
and asks it. "Melissa, do you think there's a possibility that you
took these drugs on purpose? Did you know that this amount
of drugs had the potential to kill you?"

"You mean did I try to commit suicide?"

"Yes," she answers with a warm and open expression.

I think a little. "I don't know," I say. And it's the truth. I
mean, I don't remember thinking, *I want to die.* But then
again, I must have known that taking so much could be deadly.

"Well, I think that's something we should explore a little
more, then." She says she's going to recommend that I stay
on the "unit" for some observation time, and she'll make

a referral to a psychiatrist for when I get out to see about medication.

"You think I'm depressed?" I ask.

"I think it's a possibility, Melissa," she says gently. "I think you have a lot going on in your life, and that in some ways you're doing a great job at coping, or maybe masking the sadness. But I think, given this last incident, your fights with peers, your recent breakup, and your family stress … it's enough to constitute concern."

"I don't feel depressed," I reflect.

"Depression isn't always just being sad. It comes in a lot of shapes and sizes. Sometimes it's anger or apathy. Or sometimes it shows itself through the coping mechanisms, like drugs and alcohol or criminal activity."

Now that she's talking about depression, I get scared. I don't want to take any pills. "I'm not going to do it again," I assure her, as if that will change anything now.

"That's good to hear, Melissa. I really hope not." She smiles and then gets up, indicating our time is up. "I hope to have a chance to meet with you one more time before you go home."

⟵

I'm back in my bed in the emergency room, almost asleep, and my mom is reading a magazine on the chair when the social worker returns with a youngish woman. "Hello," the ice queen social worker says, "this is Alexis, one of the CYCs from the fourth floor."

"Hi there!" she says cheerfully, waving at my mom and me.

The ice queen turns to my mom. "So, we are accepting your request for an ASU bed for Melissa here at the hospital." Then she turns to me. "We feel your ongoing risk-taking behaviour, Melissa, constitutes a significant threat to your own safety."

She moves in closer to my mom and lowers her voice slightly, as if I'm not going to hear. "Since there's a history of aggression and threatening behaviour toward others, as well as a history of high-risk activities such as sex and substance abuse and possible suicide, we feel there is just reason to admit Melissa for a few days for a period of assessment, stabilization, diagnostic evaluation, and long-term planning. That way, she can see a psychiatrist and you can have the support from the crisis team."

She didn't need to bother lowering her voice because even though I heard each word, they strung together as just one foggy blur in my ears. "Melissa." She reaches out and puts her cold, bony fingers on my thigh. "We want to keep you safe for the next few days. We're here to help you." And then, without a goodbye, she's gone.

The bubbly girl claps her hands together. "Okay. So, I know this is a strange experience for both of you. Do you have any questions so far? Anything at all?"

My mom raises her hand like she's in school. "I do. What's ASU?"

The girl laughs. "Oh, I'm so sorry. We get used to saying these acronyms all the time and forget that the whole world doesn't speak our language. ASU is Acute Support Unit, which is upstairs on the psychiatry ward. They take someone like Melissa for a few days of observation and assessment. Anything else? Please feel free to ask."

My mom shakes her head.

"Okay. So, Melissa. I'll take you to your room, where you'll be for a few days. I'm sure you're happy to get out of this place. Your room will be much more private. Do you have everything?"

I nod and motion to the plastic bag on the bed that my mother brought for me, which I haven't even gone through yet.

"Great! Then let's go," she says, picking up the bag.

We follow her. I'll go anywhere, even the morgue, to get out of the chaos of the emergency room.

"Where are my other clothes? My jeans?" I ask when we're in the elevator. I'm standing among a bunch of people and all I'm wearing is a flimsy hospital gown.

"I took them home to wash," my mom answers.

"Don't worry, we'll be giving you another groovy gown to wear anyway," the girl interjects, winking at me. I fake smile back. There's something about her happiness that makes it seem inappropriate to be sombre.

On the fourth floor, we walk down several corridors, past a security guard, and through a door that the girl has to swipe her card to unlock. "First, I'll show you your room." We follow her past a nurses' station with a ratty fake Christmas tree in front of it and down a wide hallway of patient rooms with half-opened doors I don't bother looking into. We turn into 443.

It's a basic hospital room. Bare. A curtainless window overlooking another building. A bed with sheets. A chair. A sink. A bathroom. No pictures on the walls. The only mark of human life is the piece of paper stuck to the cupboard door with rules that the girl puts her finger to and starts to read off, though I get only bits of it—no music, no phone calls, no visitors past eight.

The girl—I can't remember her name—unlocks the cupboard and starts to lay out the contents of my plastic bag. "Everything is locked up, Melissa. I know it seems harsh, but due to the nature of your admission, it's important that we help you keep safe. If you need something, you just let me know." She continues to lay out the rest of the contents—my hairbrush, face cream … She arranges the articles in a long, tidy row, lining the edges up so perfectly you could lay a ruler down.

Even my tampons? What am I going to do, hang myself with the tampon string? Or maybe plug it down my throat? I think this but don't say it aloud, because I just don't have the energy to argue. And in a way, I just don't care. They can do whatever the fuck they want with me. I just don't care.

"Okay, you'll need to shower now." She turns to my mom, who's been uncommonly silent this whole time. "And while she's doing that, maybe you could fill out some paperwork for us? Just basic info, but we do need a list of immediate family members' numbers that Melissa's allowed to call." She turns back to me. "All your calls will be monitored. Someone will be holding another phone to listen in to make sure you're staying safe. It's just our policy."

Whatever. I just head toward the washroom like she's telling me to do.

"Oh, not in there. We'll go to the common washroom for the first shower. Ms. Sullivan, I'll show you the nurses' station where you can get the papers, so it's probably good that you say goodbye now until tomorrow."

My mom looks at me all sympathetic, and approaches like she's going to hug me. "Call me if you need anything," she says. I keep my gaze down, let her hold me but don't hug back. Instead, I just turn to follow Alexis to the shower room.

⌒

There are three shower stalls in the washroom, with strange dwarf curtains that only rise waist high. I wait for her to go, but she just stands there. "Sorry, I need to be here. We want to make sure you haven't brought anything in with you. I know it's uncomfortable. I won't stand and stare, but I do have to be present."

Whatever. So I undress and get in the shower. I'm given some liquid soap and shampoo, and I turn my back so I can hide at least half of me. And I should probably care more, but I don't really. I just shower and wash and turn off the faucet and dry off with a towel and put on the ugly thin yellow gown that has no drawstrings 'cause apparently I'd hang myself with those too. It's huge and drapes off my shoulders.

The girl passes me my underwear after she inspects them in front of me. "My bra?" I ask, holding out my hand.

"Sorry, I can't give it to you. It's underwire. You need to ask your mom for a sports bra or tank top with support."

Whatever. I walk past her, my feet still wet against the cold concrete floor. "Here!" She passes me paper booties that I obediently slip on. Then I follow her back to my room, get into my bed and under the sheet. I look outside. It's already dark and it's only about six P.M. I hate winter. I see a light turn off in the office window across the street. Then I stare up at the ceiling. Eyes open, but seeing nothing.

⌒

The girl appears beside my bed. "Lights go off at 9:45. You're on 'constant,' which means constant watch. That means we need to watch you at all times to make sure you're safe — whether you're in your room, in the washroom, or in the common room. It feels a little awkward for both of us, but we have to do it. If you want some privacy, just let me know and I'll stay at the door. My name is Alexis, in case you don't remember."

I look over at her when she's finished talking, but I don't say anything because really, there is nothing in my head to say.

"So. Do you want time alone or do you want some company? We could play cards or something."

"I don't care."

"Or we could listen to music?"

"It doesn't matter. You choose."

"No, you make the choice, Melissa. What would you like?"

"Whatever. It really doesn't matter."

She smiles. "Okay. I'll leave you alone. I'll just be outside if you change your mind." She walks out to the doorway and sits down on a chair. I stare at her a minute longer, wondering if she'll be sitting like that all night.

I stare back up at the ceiling. My eyelids click when I blink, like those plastic baby dolls with glassy eyes and frozen faces. I feel stoned. My head is cloudy and it's hard to focus on any one thought. I fall in and out of sleep for some time.

Click. Clack. Click.

The fluorescent light flickers off. I don't know if Alexis turned it off or if it just goes off automatically. I lie awake for a long time. The announcements blare through the loudspeaker in my room. So and so to come to the nurses' desk. Something something about line two. Code red, blue, purple, whatever.

I half sleep all night. Part of me, my body, tosses and turns under the tightly tucked-in sheets. The other part, my mind, sits all night on the edge of the bed, rocking back and forth, trying to squeeze out a thought as to how the hell I ended up here.

Fifty-Two

It's like being dead. Don't they get that? It's like they give you exactly what you wanted before you came in here. They give you non-existence.

In this hollow bone of a room, I am rid of all responsibility. All contact. All choice. I have no voice or purpose throughout the day. Even my body isn't mine.

I'm sure the world I used to live in has gone on without me. It's like I don't even matter. Right now, my friends are going to school. The same people are on my morning bus. FLOW 93.5 is playing the top seven at seven. Fortune is texting one of his many girlfriends. Eric is seeing a client. Jess is staring in a mirror, fixing her face for the zillionth time since she woke up. My mother is trying to squeeze on her size-six jeans and tie an elastic band around the waist button. Life goes on and on and on ... and that tiny bump of me that existed inside the tiniest fold of time has already been smoothed over.

And maybe that's why I don't care about anything. Because I (all that I know as "me") am dead and this body is just a facade of the person I used to be. If it were the old me, I'd be arguing and fighting and planning my escape. I'd erupt in anger if someone had to watch me shit and shower and dress and sleep. I should be sad thinking about what happened, or about my pathetic life, or about Michael. But now it's like I'm here but not here. And this person they are watching over is only a mass of energy held together by skin. Like I'm caught in some unthinking place, before birth and after death, some realm of existence where not only do you not care about anything, you just "do not."

My guard today, a pregnant lady with long black hair, suggests we go to the common room, where there are a TV and games. I don't necessarily want to go, but I have no real reason not to, so I get out of bed and follow her. That's where I see the others: three girls about my age watching music videos and two boys about ten years old playing a board game. In the hallway I had passed a couple more people: one really, really tall girl whose gown is like a miniskirt and a guy with bad acne.

I wonder if they're all in here because they tried to kill themselves. They all look a little nuts, but maybe it's just 'cause I expect them to be. I think of the book *One Flew Over the Cuckoo's Nest* that we read in class. I imagine us escaping out a window and hijacking a bus. I'd be Jack Nicholson for sure. Or Angelina Jolie in *Girl, Interrupted*. Except maybe not. Not anymore. Maybe, right now, I'd just be Chief 'cause I haven't spoken to anyone basically in two days.

The pregnant lady makes me play cards with her. We play a mindless game called Skip-bo. And then she teaches me crazy eights. At some point, two staffers enter with a girl about my age. She looks like a wreck. It's as if she was normal a while ago and then something really terrible happened. Anyway, they all take a seat and the staff talk to her like she's a baby. They have a plate full of food on the table and they actually spoon-feed her. "Come on, Anna, just one more bite? Yeah! Atta girl. Great job!"

I can't help but stare. It freaks me out how weird it is, how she can't even feed herself. What the hell happened to her?

"Your turn," the pregnant lady says, drawing me back to the game of crazy eights, which I suppose is a funny name for a game to play in a mental ward.

I slap down my last card, winning the game.

"Hey! You won!" she exclaims, but I really couldn't give a shit.

Fifty-Three

I have a busy morning the next day. First I see the psychiatrist one more time. She asks me more questions about my mom and about living at home. And then we talk about Michael and Fortune and everything else, but I still don't say anything about what happened with Giovanni. It's an okay conversation, but really, what can she solve in one hour? At the end of the session she tells me about a psychiatrist appointment she's set up for me once I'm out. I thank her, for what I don't know, and then leave. Alexis is outside the door when I open it and escorts me to another office by the nurses' station, where we wait for a "family meeting" with the ice queen social worker.

I lean up against the cold wall, far away from Alexis so that I can think. I know I should have told the shrink about Giovanni since what happened is probably what fucked me up so badly. But what I did was so absolutely shameful I can never tell anyone. Not even Ally or Jessica. I can't bring myself to think about it, let alone talk about it. Does everyone need therapy over one mistake? One moment?

Icchh. I shudder each time the memory creeps into my head. I just can't believe what I did, even if I was high. Of all the things to remember about that night, this has to be the most clear?

I decide I will do my own therapy. I will chase the image from my mind each time it arises, until finally, one day, it just won't come. Like a call-forward command on a phone, the thought will eventually be redirected without me being aware of it. If there's a scratch in my brain causing the memory of my hands on Giovanni to repeat over and over again, why can't I record over it with another memory to be stuck on?

So each time the image pops up, I will chase it away with something beautiful. I will think of Bradley sitting on our old kitchen linoleum floor. In his hand is a string I tied around a plastic yellow duck. He is madly snapping the string, making the duck fly spastically around, until it hits him in the face, but instead of crying, he just looks up at me and laughs at the shock of it.

The door of the office opens and I'm surprised to see that my mom is already inside. She looks at me and smiles, but it's just a fake smile. I can tell she's not okay. The Ice Queen greets me and asks me to sit down. She tells us that she has an update from the crisis management team. Apparently they say there are several options from this point forward. She explains all of this to my mom, as if I'm not even in the room. I don't know what has happened. It's like suddenly the two of them are a team against me.

When she's done, Ice Queen finally looks over at me. "Your mother really cares about you, Melissa. She's been doing some hard work here with us. We have gone over all the options, one of which is you being placed in a temporary care facility, such as a group home. If you are refusing treatment and your mom is unable to control your behaviour, it's really our only option. But your mom feels that if you are co-operative, it's possible she could have you back at home with some community support ..."

"I can't do it anymore, Melissa. Especially not now," my mom interjects, and puts her hand on her belly. Her voice starts to quiver. "You almost died ... I can't live with all this stress. You not coming home. The drugs. Your temper. I just can't do it."

"Then don't," I say matter-of-factly, staring down at my lap. My words aren't angry, just tired. "I know where I'll live."

"Where's that?" the social worker asks.

"At a friend's place. Allison's friend. This guy. He has a room he'll rent out."

"Oh, God ..." My mom buries her head in her hands.

"Melissa, I'm afraid that's not an option at this time. It wouldn't be a good decision, especially when you're in this state of mind. We want you to be safe. Your mom, if she wants, can sign something to make sure you go directly into care. Now, I don't think that's what either one of you wants. So if we can take this time to work something out practically, I think you both can find common ground. Shall we try?"

I nod my head.

⌒

I trail my mom down the corridor, taking my time. There's nowhere to go but my room, so why hurry? My mom keeps ahead of me, and I feel like she's mad or something. It's not like her to be so strict.

Inside my room, her mood picks up a bit. She unwraps a bouquet of flowers that is sitting on my bedside table and shows them to me, pointing at the little attached teddy bear. "Crystal bought these for you. Just to cheer things up a bit," she says, bringing the bouquet to her nose and deeply inhaling.

"She's real worried about you." She takes a small glass vase out of her bag and heads toward the washroom.

"Are we being kicked out?" I ask her, seemingly randomly, once she's out of sight. I'm thinking about Giovanni and wondering if he'd tell anyone. Part of me hopes we are kicked out, because I don't ever want to see him again.

"Of what?"

"The apartment."

"No." She peeks her head around the door frame and looks at me as if I've just asked if she's from the moon. "Why would we be kicked out?"

I shrug my shoulders. "I don't know. No money to pay the rent?"

She disappears back into the washroom and starts to run the tap to fill the vase.

"I got a job!" she shouts over the rush of water. "Assistant to a tax guy. Not bad pay. Totally flexible hours. I can probably even do some work on the sly when I'm on my maternity leave."

My mom returns to the room holding the vase and puts it on my windowsill. I instantly smell the fragrance. About two seconds later, Alexis appears, her hands clasped together like she's praying for forgiveness. "I'm sorry, Ms. Sullivan, Melissa can't receive any gifts while she's here. And she can't have the vase—it's glass."

"Oh … okay." My mom fumbles and quickly picks up the vase. I've never seen her so obedient.

"She can keep the teddy bear, but we have to lock it up."

"A teddy bear?" my mom questions, then immediately backs off. "Okay. I'll put it in her room at home." She looks a little hurt. She was already told yesterday by Alexis that she couldn't put up all the holiday decorations she had brought with her. A big bagful, that I'm sure cost her a lot.

For a second, I get a flash of Bradley. His hospital room. Full of flowers and Christmas ornaments and cookie boxes and Cellophane-wrapped gift baskets. It's funny, I haven't thought once about the fact that it's my first time in a hospital since he died. And about how all this must be weird on a whole other level for my mom.

Alexis goes back to her guard chair at the doorway and my mom sits awkwardly on the plastic cushioned bench for a bit. I sit on the edge of my bed and stare at the wall. I feel my mom staring at me for some time, and then I hear her pick up a magazine and flip through it.

I'm thinking about Michael. I imagine what he'd say if he saw me now. He'd probably be relieved he dumped me when he did. But then I shake my head to lose him from my mind, because now, thinking of him makes me feel a little sick to my stomach. I'm embarrassed at how pathetic I've been over losing him. And there's this faint, faint whisper inside my head that's saying maybe my overdose was also about him.

"Well, I guess I'll get going," my mom says, interrupting my thoughts.

"Bye," I say blankly, not lifting my gaze from the wall.

She gets up, kisses me on the forehead, stops at the doorway to talk to Alexis for a bit, and then leaves.

Later, Alexis convinces me to go eat my dinner in the common room with the others. I do it for her really, 'cause I prefer to just eat alone in my room. There are four other patients in there: the two younger boys and one new girl, older than me, with her blue gown halfway down her shoulders, almost showing her whole boobs. At the end of the table, looking totally nuts, is the pimply, skinny guy I saw yesterday. I can tell he's been here a long time because the two staff around him look exhausted and are barely containing their annoyance.

Alexis gets my cardboard plate off the trolley. She opens the Styrofoam container and unveils my gourmet meal: macaroni and cheese and dessert. "It's been opened," I remark, referring to the cutlery package.

"Oh, it's okay. They just take out the knives," she answers.

Whatever. I eat red Jell-O dessert first. It's like swallowing live *kid-ness*. I can see why children like it so much, all jiggly on the spoon and smooth down your throat. I think of Bradley and me eating it for dessert, and then Bradley squeezing it out between his teeth like he was bleeding, and our mom yelling at him.

"Yaah … yeahh … heeahhh …" This loud, ugly voice trips me on my warm and fuzzy stroll down memory lane. Psycho boy is flinging his food onto the floor. Not in a silly way, but in an angry way. Instead of yelling at him, the staff just ask him to stop and then pick up the food. But of course he keeps going and going until everyone in the room is paying attention to him. I try to return to my Jell-O eating, but he does it again. "Yahhhh … oooohhhiiii … ha … ha … ha!"

"Fuckin' crazy," I mutter under my breath, and put down my Jell-O bowl. I push away my chair, get up, put my hands on my waist, and stare him down, the words filling my mouth like the Jell-O I just shoved in it. *Hey, cuckoo bird, why don't you shut the fuck up so we can eat our shit food in peace, will ya?* But I don't say it, because they'd probably put me in a straitjacket or something, so instead I head toward the room, my shadow Alexis following me.

As we walk down the hall, Alexis speaks to me in a bitchy tone that sounds strange coming from her. "Listen, I know you're upset, but next time you can't just pick up and leave like that. You need to tell me where you're going."

"He should be responsible for his own behaviour. He can't poison the whole room like that." I raise my voice as we pass the nurses' station so they can all hear me. "You should not let him in there. It's so selfish. I mean, if you're nuts, you shouldn't impose it on others."

"I see your point," Alexis says calmly, "but this is a hospital. This is where he should be to get help. It's not like he's in a restaurant and interrupting a fine meal. This is where he belongs, Melissa."

I stop outside my door and turn to her. "If *that* belongs here, then *I* don't belong here."

And I realize right then that I'm coming back—that angry, agitated, unrested me has returned from the dead like one of those psycho killers in movies who keep getting up after being stabbed a thousand times. It's as if someone has turned the tap and released the hot water that's now filling me back up. I feel the heat inside. I feel the pressure. I feel something creaking and groaning.

And for some reason, I get all scared, because part of me wants to remain a zombie. I go into my room, lie down on my bed, and stare blankly at the ceiling, trying to dumb down my mood and return to my coma state. But it's like that whispery, smoky ghost is slipping away and I can't reach out and grab her—my fingers just run right through.

Fifty-Four

My mom and I meet again with the social worker in her nondescript, spacious office on the fifth floor. She sits behind her big, empty desk while we swivel on black upholstered chairs that look like ice cream cones. Perfect for an ice queen, I suppose. The walls are painted a sedating eggplant purple, and a large painting of an ocean sunset threatens to put us all into hypnotic sleep.

"I'd like to talk to you about you going home, Melissa," she says.

"I'm getting out?" Which is only a thrilling idea because I'm so goddamn bored in here.

"That's correct," she says, void of expression. It's not as if her face, like some people's, is too tight to smile. Her absence of smile seems forced, as if she believes the mere parting of her lips would be a crack in her authority. "The psychiatrist thinks that we can go ahead and discuss a discharge plan. As long as we have the proper care in place and you're on board, then we think you'll be ready and a Form 3 won't be necessary. That means you don't need to go to a residential care facility. Your mom has been participating in several sessions with me and she's prepared to take you back under certain conditions. We have lots of support in place for you and your mom, but you are a major player on the team, Melissa. You are the quarterback. We can't do it unless we have your full commitment."

"Okay." There's something really unfair about all of this. I'm almost naked under a thin hospital gown, braless, and grounded by flimsy paper slippers. My brain is doped up with some kind of medication and my body is still shaky from withdrawal.

"You already have some good supports in place. You see your counsellor Eric each week, and I hear you're doing really well at the day treatment school program. I'll be honest and tell you our team really debated about a residential substance abuse program, but your mom and your counsellor thought they could work on this with you. It is, however, an option, and for the most part our team recommends it. If you choose to remain at home, the hospital Crisis Support Team will provide two home visits while you're waiting to set up with the social worker from Everwood Family Services. Your social worker will continue to provide in-home family support once a week. And …" Ice Queen turns to my mom, who has cowered under her whip.

"You will have a ten o'clock curfew, and if you break it," my mom says in a firm voice, "I have agreed that the residential treatment plan will be reactivated. This is it, Melissa. This is the end. You hear me, Melissa?"

I don't respond because there's really nothing happening in my head right now. I don't even have any fierce words on the tip of my tongue waiting to be swallowed or spat out. I just keep staring at my lap and twirling my ring like an idiot.

"Melissa?" Ice Queen joins in.

I ignore her voice because I figure she'll just plow ahead like every other time we've talked to her.

"Melissa? Can you look at me?"

I raise my eyes and feel myself starting to get annoyed. Why the fuck do I have to look into her dead eyes?

"You have a lot in place here to help you, Melissa. It's up to you now to take advantage of it, and get back on track. From the short time I've known you, I think that's entirely possible. I think you have a bright future ahead of you." She winks at me and for the first time opens her mouth to a thin smile. "Right?"

I stare at her for a second. Everything was okay until that last statement. Why do adults have to diminish everything by feeling they need to end meetings with a false positive? It's so selfish. They say it not because they believe it, but because it helps them feel some kind of accomplishment when they walk away. Like they've done their job. But what do they leave behind?

It's like when teachers tell Tyler that he should be a lawyer because he's good at arguing, but meanwhile he can't pass grade nine. No one wants to say he's stupid, or that he's probably going to end up in jail like his brother, so they fill his head with these stupid dreams until he's eighteen, with no credits and totally messed up for life. I say, tell the truth, squash the dream, and stop with the second chances.

A bright future ahead of me? "Right," Echo says.

Within two hours, I'm packed and ready to go home.

"Well ... don't take this the wrong way, but I hope I don't see you again," Alexis says to me, smiling and unlocking the cupboard. She passes me my plastic bag.

"Yeah, me too," I say. I'm a little sad to leave her because she's turned out to be pretty cool. "But thanks. If you weren't around, I'd have killed myself with boredom. Ha ha."

Alexis rolls her eyes and gives me a hug that I'm not prepared for, so I barely have time to bring my arms around her before she quickly pulls away.

"Peace," I wave, and then lead my mom down the hallway, past the security guard, and toward the elevators.

In some ways, I'm happy to leave the hospital. I was bored out of my mind, I hated wearing the oversized gown, and I couldn't sleep well at night. On the other hand, it was actually not so bad being there. In a messed-up way, it was good to be told what to do all the time because that way you don't have the stress of choosing, and then the stress of having made the wrong decision. I can't explain it. It's like being held really, really tight. Not the caring way someone holds a baby, but more like the restraining way they would use to calm down a hysterical person. They hold and hold and hold until you calm down and your breathing returns and your muscles relax. And even though it's forceful and you fight it, you actually want it, because you know deep down you're being protected from yourself.

It's the same way cats get when I pin them down on the examining table with my medieval metal-chain-armoured arms. After some panic and fighting, they just relax into it, as if they know it's for their own good.

It's like that.

I can feel a change. Something loosens. Something trusts. And something lets go.

Fifty-Five

For the whole way home, I lie down in the back seat of the car and pretend I'm sleeping because I don't know what to say to my mom. I feel like she knows everything about me now and I'm naked in front of her, and it's hard to get angry at someone when you're naked. The moment we get out of the car, I trail her like a nervous duckling, almost tripping over her heels. We stop to get the mail on the way up from the underground garage. "Another bill," she comments to herself, not even acknowledging me. For once in her life, she's at a loss for words. There's a new distance between us. Some kind of gap that neither one of us knows how to cross. It's like someone pulled us out of the nasty rut we were in, shook us hard, and then set us back down again in our roles, all wobbly and disoriented. And now our mouths stay shut because we're too busy focusing on trying to regain our balance and pinpoint our surroundings.

Just before we get to our apartment door, my mom stops. I walk past her because I figure she's looking for her keys, but she doesn't follow. I turn, wondering what she's doing.

She stands there looking at me, sort of lost and pitiful. That new tough person I saw in the hospital is gone.

"What?" I ask.

She sighs, throws one hand up in the air in surrender, and says, "I feel like I gave this to you. If you do have depression, I feel like it came from me." She brings her hand quickly up to her eyes to cover them. She's crying.

"Oh, Mom …" I move toward her. "You didn't give it to me. They don't even know for sure that I have it." I feel like I'm talking about the measles or something. I reach my hand out and hold her shoulder because I don't know what else to do. I'm sort of going through the motions because I still feel a little numb in my head. And now that she's said it, I think it might be true. Maybe she *did* give it to me. But it's not her fault. It would be stupid to think that.

She moves closer and gives me a hug, sniffing her snotty nose into my jacket. Then she quickly pulls away. "Whew!" she says, waving her hands in front of her eyes like she's air-drying them. "Okay. Sorry. It's not about me!" She laughs awkwardly, like she's embarrassed about her breakdown.

Wow. I feel I'm on another planet. My mother just said, "It's not about me"? Did I hear right? Someone must have said something to her at the hospital. Maybe Ice Queen was not so awful after all.

My mom pulls at my hand and leads me onward. "This is hard for you. Coming home. I'm sorry. Let's go in."

She opens the apartment door and we walk through.

⌒

Crystal is sitting at our kitchen table. There are fast-food bags crumpled around her. She looks like crap, as if she's been up for days. She smiles when she sees me and puts her hands together in her stupid "Namaste" yoga salutation pose. "Glad you're home, Sweetie," she says as I pass by.

"Thanks," I reply sullenly, and keep walking. I pass through the living room, now decorated for Christmas, complete with dangling tinsel streamers and a fancy store-bought Christmas tree. It looks good, but all I care about is being back in my room. My own bed. My own sheets. My own pillow. My own music. My own phone. I find my journal sitting out on my desk where I left it, and I immediately panic. I'm sure my mom read it, and Crystal too. I just know it. I open it to the last entry, the one I wrote before I went out that last night. I don't even remember what I said, so I read it with new eyes.

Dearest Michael,

You know why I like "The Lady of Shalott" so much? Why I read it to you all the time? It's because she is me. We are the same. We are both stuck in this tower. Cursed. We both watch life pass by, unable to join in. We both fall in love with someone on the other side (that's you), but we know it's impossible to ever be with him, in that life.

And so we must die.

But really, the tragedy in the poem is not Lady Shalott's death. It's all about that one line: "Lancelot mused a little space, he said she has a lovely face. God in his mercy lent her grace, the Lady of Shalott." It's that small moment of regret, Michael, that makes her story tragic.

It's all about what could have been, and what can never be. You will have that regret, Michael. You will make my story tragic. And that will be the curse YOU will live with.

Yours forever & never more,
Melissa

What the hell? What was I thinking? How sappy. I feel so stupid. I read the letter like five times, trying to remember writing it that night before I went out with Ally and got really shit-faced. Was I already high? Maybe it was intentional—maybe I did want to die. It makes me feel sick. Disgusted with myself.

My story isn't beautiful or tragic. It's just another story about another cursed girl living a shitty life.

Fifty-Six

I spend the next few days in my room. Not because I'm hiding. I just feel like being alone. I don't call any of my friends. I don't know if I ever want to call them. I reread a couple of my favourite books. I write in my journal, filling it up with everything that has happened to me in the past few months. I sort through all my clothes and chuck out about half of them. I even clean under my bed and find a souvenir hairball from Ralph. My mom checks in on me a million times a day, asking me how I feel, but she doesn't force me to talk. Instead, she rents me movies, gets me pizza and anything I want. I stay in my pyjamas and I don't answer my phone. And it's like I'm seven years old again, staying home with the flu. My mom feels like "a mom." And it all feels kinds of nice.

After a few days, she tells me she wants me to go to our family doctor, right after she takes me to the psychiatrist on Wednesday afternoon. "I want everything checked," she says. *"Everything."*

"They already checked me at the hospital, blood and everything … I'm okay," I protest. I know she's talking about the guys I've been with and how I didn't use a condom the past few times. I guess hearing about how many there were kind of freaked her out.

"No argument about this one, Mel."

I don't have the energy to put up a fight, but I do tell her I'll go only to a clinic where no one knows me. So after I get loaded up with depression medication from the shrink, she takes me to some drop-in clinic downtown and sits with me in the waiting room full of pamphlets on every possible disease you could ever get from having sex, which just makes you terrified about being there, and if my mom wasn't with me I'd run out the door.

In the examination room, the nurse talks to me, asking the sickest questions. How many partners? How much unprotected sex? Anal sex? Oral sex? Use of sex toys? Blah blah blah. I feel like a total slut. Then she tells me about all the tests—HIV, gonorrhea, everything. By the time she's done talking, I'm so scared I want to throw up, because even though you learn all that stuff at school, you just don't think anything bad will happen to you. And when you're in that little office with nowhere to go, it's like sitting before the all-knowing God of STDs and you must face up to all your stupid sins.

"Was it okay?" my mom asks on the way home. She's driving real slow because it's the first snowfall of the winter.

"Fine," I answer. "I feel kind of sick." I roll down the window to feel the cold air on my face. I'm thinking of all those little bits of my body I've left behind at the clinic: my blood, my fluids, my cells. I think about how they hold the truth to my past. And how, even if you want to forget your mistakes, the body will hold on to your secrets forever.

Deep, deep in your cells, the truth will always be there, threatening to be revealed.

Fifty-Seven

When Sisyphus almost reaches the top of the hill, I wish that for a second, just a split second, maybe even just one-millithousandth of a second, there could be some sense of accomplishment. I wish Sisyphus could pretend his task is almost complete or that a reward for his pain will soon follow. But as the story goes, before these thoughts can even begin to take root in his mind, the rock starts to creak and tremble and then it thunders downward. And, of course, he has to run after it. Down, down, down to the very bottom, where he stands in the muck. Breathless. Staring back up at a peak that looks so damn far, far away. And there is no choice but to place his palms against the gritty rock, push, and go back up again.

↩

Up. Up. Up I go.
    I wake.
    I shower.
    I brush my teeth.
    I dress.

I eat two pieces of toast.

I follow my mom to the car.

I hold my hand up to shade my eyes, paining from the bright sun.

Ever since the OD, I feel like I'm this glass doll that everyone can peer into. Everyone knows my secrets now: my mom, Crystal, everyone at the hospital. I'm embarrassed to see Eric because he will know all of this too, even about Michael. But my mother is driving me to the appointment and she told me she's going to take me straight to the door, so I'll have no choice but to go.

Of course, Eric is cool about everything. He doesn't make me feel like an idiot. He tells me I don't have to go into everything that happened because I signed that form at the hospital and they updated him. Even though he does nothing to make me feel guilty, I do. I don't take off my winter hat when I'm in his office. It's so low on my forehead it almost covers my eyes. I wish I could disappear right under it. I bring my fingers up to my mouth and start biting my nails, almost non-existent now. "I'm sorry I never told you."

"What's that?"

I can barely force the words up my throat. I haven't used this voice, my real voice, *Melissa's* voice, in so long. I decide right then and there, no matter how hard it is, I'll stop being Echo with Eric. I mean, I'm not ready to give her up entirely, but it doesn't make sense for me to keep shutting out my counsellor. He's proven I can trust him. And if I don't start with someone I can trust, who will I ever tell my real feelings to? "I'm sorry I never told you about my boyfriend. About Michael."

"Oh. It's okay, Melissa. You don't need to tell me everything.

You had reasons for not telling me at the time. I can respect that."

I stare down at my fingers, inspecting them as I speak. It's difficult being honest! Even though I want to put Michael behind me, I still feel compelled to explain, because I feel like I was lying all this time, sending him down the wrong path and wasting his time. "Well ... it was a while ago. I didn't want to say. 'Cause he was older. But that's why I was so sad for so long. That's why I'm such a wreck. I think that's what was happening to me."

"Thanks for telling me, Melissa. It helps me understand a little better what's happening with you. Love is an amazing thing, isn't it? But when you lose it, it can be so devastating. Do you want to tell me about him?"

"No!" I say decisively. "I'm finished with him."

"Okay," he says casually, nodding his head.

I look away. A few seconds of silence pass like hours. I feel like an idiot for being so weak about a guy. Eric clears his throat. I'm staring into the goldfish bowl. Waiting. I can't look at him. I tap on the fishbowl and pretend to be interested in Amphitrite, waiting for him to speak again.

"The psychiatrist talked to you about depression? She gave you some medication? How's that feeling? I know it's early. You may not notice any change for some time."

I'm relieved he's switched the subject, even though I know he'll probably come back to it during another session. I shrug my shoulders. "I feel okay. I mean, I haven't been doing anything, so it's hard to tell."

He tells me he knows a really good psychiatrist I could see regularly whom he knows I'd like. He says he could make an appointment, just to talk. I don't have to commit to anything.

"You think a pill can make someone happy?" I ask.

"No. It won't necessarily make you happy. But it might help

you better deal with life circumstances, put you on a level playing field. Help you see things a little more clearly. And help you deal with problems. Which can lead to being happier."

"Hmm."

There's a new, awkward silence in the room. It just doesn't feel the same between us.

"You had us all scared, Melissa. I want you to know I'm always here to help."

"I know. I'm sorry. I don't know what my problem is." I'm still looking downward, hiding under my wool toque. I just don't feel like letting him see my face now.

"Well, we've spent a lot of time over the past couple of years talking about your anger, where it comes from."

"I don't feel angry anymore. I think it's gone."

"That's good," Eric says positively. "But sometimes the same feelings that cause the anger can cause a great sadness too. I feel like there's something we should have talked about more before. I'm hoping we can start talking about it today, if you're feeling comfortable enough. I don't want to push you."

"I'm fine."

"I'm wondering if you can talk to me a little about how you felt when Bradley died."

"What do you mean?"

"Well, death is pretty complicated. People have all sorts of responses to it, depending on the circumstances. Of course, there's sadness. But sometimes there are also other feelings that are surprising. What happened after Bradley died?"

"You already know this. We talked about it before," I say. "My mom got totally depressed. We lost our apartment and we stayed in that shelter for a bit."

"Yes, that was a really tough time."

"No, it was fun," I say sarcastically. A stupid comment requires a stupid response.

"How did you feel about your mom then, do you remember?"

I shrug my shoulders.

"Were you angry?"

"A bit."

"Do you know why?"

"'Cause we had to live in a shelter."

"Was there anyone you were mad at?"

"My mom," I say quickly. "But it wasn't her fault. She had a mental breakdown."

"Your mind knows it wasn't her fault, but your emotions can have their own reaction. It's okay to feel angry. It's natural to feel somewhat resentful, at the same time as feeling sympathetic. Try to take yourself back to that twelve-year-old girl. Close your eyes. Imagine her. Do you remember a feeling of sadness or anger or apathy or …?"

I close my eyes and think about it for a second. I picture a skinny-legged, younger me in jean shorts and a blue T-shirt. A tomboy. Straggly hair. No socks. Runners. "I don't know. Anger, I guess."

"At who?"

I start to get annoyed with him. We already went over this. "My mom. For messing up."

"Do you think you were more mad at your mom or at Bradley?"

"Bradley?" I look at Eric, horrified at the question. "You can't blame a kid for dying. That's the worst possible thing in the world to say. It would make me the Devil or something."

"It would make you human, Melissa. You're human. You were a kid. You had a right to be taken care of. If life crumbled after he died and you were a kid, you'd naturally blame him a bit for that."

"Hmmm," I respond, half interested. *Was* I mad at Bradley? "Anyway, it's not a big deal to me now."

"No. Probably not in your mind. But sometimes feelings or experiences, when they are planted inside you, can be seeds that grow in many different directions. These seeds can affect all sorts of decisions and beliefs in your life without you even realizing it."

"Hmmm," I respond again, which is how I answer when he says something that might be good and I need time to think about it. Eric knows I'm not the kind of person to just jump into an idea. I need to be alone first to contemplate it, then come back to him and talk some more.

"If it's ever something you want to talk to your mom about, I'd really encourage you."

"Why would I talk to her about that? She'd think I was a total bitch."

Eric gets all serious and sincere. "I don't think so, Melissa. I really don't. I think she'd understand and I think there would be some beginning of healing between you two. Just think about it."

"Okay," I say dismissively, but after I leave the session I go to the washroom, open the windows, sit on the counter, and have a smoke to give myself time to think about what he said before I meet my mom in the waiting room.

Eric, as usual, might be right about Bradley. I had never really thought about feeling angry toward him because my thoughts were always rerouted to the sorrow of his death. But if I make myself think about it now, maybe there is a point to Eric's theory. Maybe I *am* still mad at Bradley for dying and wrecking our family. And our future. And for messing up my mom, forever. And it is possible that I put all that anger toward my mom because she's easier to blame. And maybe that's why, no matter how hard my mom tries to make things work between us, I always end up pushing her away.

Someone knocks on the door. I suppose I've taken a long

time. I butt out my smoke and flick it out the window. I spray the air freshener and then squeeze through the door, not looking at the lady waiting outside.

My mom is too busy texting on her cellphone to notice me when I walk into the waiting room. I step right up to her so our knees are almost touching. She raises her head and smiles. "How was it?"

"Good," I say. I take a look around the room. There are a few people waiting—two adults and a guy about my age. "It's good I came."

"Oh," she responds, obviously surprised at my positive demeanour.

I want to say something nice to her. Something like "Thank you" or "Sorry for all this" or something like that. But I'd feel like an idiot being so sappy. And the other people in the waiting room would hear me. And the words just won't come out of my mouth. "Do you want to go to Starbucks?" I ask her instead, which is her most favourite place to chill out in. She knows I hate it there, so if I'm offering to go, it's because I'm trying to be nice.

"Sounds good," she says, rising quickly from her seat and putting her arm around my shoulder as we walk out of the room and into the main foyer.

Fifty-Eight

A few days later, I wake up with the decision in my head that I will go back to school. Snap! Just like that. For some reason, on this particular morning, I suddenly feel like putting on some makeup.

I walk into class and it's like nothing ever happened to me. Ms. Dally welcomes me back and gives me my work. No one looks at me strange, but I keep to myself because I don't know if the other students know about what happened.

Later in the morning, the youth worker, Sheila, pulls me out of class to talk to me in the couch room. She tells me none of the other students know why I was away and that it's up to me to tell them if I want to. She says she was sorry to hear about everything that happened, and that she and Ms. Dally want to help me get back on track. She tells me she's always available to talk if I'm feeling upset. I tell her I'm all talked out and that I've been speaking to Eric and a shrink and my mother.

"Okay. But I do have to talk to you about the overdose. About how much you took that night, and the dangers associated with mixing all those things."

"I don't want to go over all of it. I just want to forget about it," I object, starting to get annoyed.

"I'm not saying we have to go over everything that happened, Mel. I'm just saying we'll make a plan for next time."

"There won't be a next time."

"I sure hope not. But life is unpredictable. Let's just think of a plan. It will take only a few minutes."

She opens the binder that's sitting on the table in front of her and begins. She's being nice about it, and I don't think I can do anything to get out of it, so I just go along with her plan. We start with how I felt before I went out that night with my friends. "Were you upset?"

"Yeah."

"Did you know you would be using?"

"Yeah." I look away, biting my lower lip. "I already went over all this at the hospital."

"I know. Just bear with me."

So we make a plan for the next time I feel that upset and want to get totally wrecked out of my mind. We write down strategies I could use to avoid turning to drugs when I'm feeling so crazy. Things like making a phone call to a friend or a helpline or even the hospital. "Delay going out as long as possible. Even one hour. And if you do choose to go out and use, never ever mix, especially sedatives with alcohol."

She makes me write a list of personal max amounts I won't go over, no matter what. I have to do it for each drug: alcohol, K, E, coke. "You need to draw a line, right now. A line that you will never ever cross in terms of your use. You might not stick to it, but if you clearly think about it ahead of time, you'll be more likely to reconsider in the moment."

Just when I think we're finished, she makes me go over all the dangers related to my high use. Like rape, drunk driving, accidents, poor judgment, blah blah blah.

Finally, she leaves me to set a substance abuse goal for the week. I plan no more than one gram a day and no alcohol. "I'm keeping weed," I announce firmly when she walks back into the room. "I need something."

"We have a harm reduction philosophy, Melissa. You don't have to stop everything. And it's your goal. It's up to you," she agrees.

I finish up with my strategies: not to hang out with friends who use, not to carry money on me, to keep seeing Eric, go straight home after school, and write in my journal when things are bothering me. When we're done, Sheila takes my sheet, follows me back into the classroom, and makes sure I put it in my binder.

Fifty-Nine

My goals are easy to keep. I stay home every night. I watch TV after school. It's not like I'm *trying* to stay away from friends or drugs, it's just that I don't want to see them or use. I feel different inside. Not necessarily better—just different. Maybe it's the depression medication, or maybe I just got scared. Whatever it is, I don't think I'll ever go back to being that old "Mel." She's gone. The fight is gone.

I almost forget about the OD until my mom sits me down at the kitchen table a few nights later. She has a folder in front of her, and she begins to lecture me about mixing drugs and E and alcohol. She draws diagrams and makes lists and gives me a ton of articles printed off the internet. And then she pushes a book on teenage drinking across the table toward me.

"My school already talked to me about this," I say. It's something new for her to do: act like a responsible parent. It's something I suppose I had always wanted her to do, but I can't take any more discussions about that night.

"I don't want the next phone call from the hospital to say you're dead." She stares down at all the papers spread across the table. She looks tired.

I feel bad for putting her through all this. I should get up and hug her or something, but I just can't bring myself to move. It's not like she's a terrible mom. Like it or not, we're in this life, this apartment, together. I suppose we're sort of stuck together. And really, she's the only one who ever stands by me no matter what.

The thing about getting older is that you sometimes realize maybe you're an idiot after all. Even more frightening is the sudden awareness of your "self" in all of the mess. Before, you were always pointing a finger outward. Everything was outward. But then you turn sixteen and all of a sudden it occurs to you that perhaps *you* are part of the problem. Perhaps these fucked-up people around you are fucked up partly *because* of you.

Apparently, when you're a little baby there's some point when you suddenly realize that your body is separate from the rest of the world. That "you" actually end at your skin, and the rest of the world begins. I think you get a similar, second realization like this when you're a teenager. Only it's not about seeing you're separate; it's understanding that stuff you do actually influences other people's lives. And then, on top of life sucking, you have to deal with the guilty burden of all that.

"I'm sorry, Mom. I'm sorry. I'm sorry about everything. I'm not going to do it again." It feels so good to finally have said it to her.

She smiles. I know my words meant a big deal to her. "You have to stop hanging out with those people," she adds.

"I will. I don't even want to see them again. I only want to see Ally or Jess. No one else." I'm sure everyone knows I overdosed, and I feel like an idiot now. I want different friends. And if I can't get different friends, I'd rather stay alone.

"I want you to take lessons or something. Maybe dance, or piano? You used to be good with music."

"Mom. We don't have a piano."

She laughs. For the first time, I notice wrinkles around her eyes. "Well, something. The flute? That's light. Anyway, you know what I mean."

"Yeah," I agree. I feel like something just happened between us. Like I've barrelled through some kind of blockade. Like I've reached out to her extended hand and let her pull me over to the other side. Her side.

Sixty

Freestyle says that to become someone new, the old person in you must first die. You have to fully let that person go. He tells me I need new friends, a new school, and a whole new way to have fun. "Believe me, kid, I've tried many, many times to start a new life. But it don't last if you don't kill that old you first. It's just too tempting to fall back."

I don't think it will be that hard for me to do. I already have a new school. It's not like any of my friends are that special to me, except for Ally and Jess. And it's not like I do anything interesting in my life, other than party at random apartments with strangers. So it's no great loss. But I know for sure there is one person I have to get out of my life forever before I can move on.

Michael,

It's crazy to be in love with someone so much that you lose yourself. The more lost you feel, the more desperately you love. There's no stopping it. Except this ... there comes a moment when you begin to hate yourself for being so pathetic. And then, it's not like the love is gone, it's just that you can't reach it in your heart anymore. And that once-unstoppable love stops right away. Just like that. Gone. And all you're left with is embarrassment and shame for the pitiful person you have become.

I let you go, Michael. You are free.

And so am I.

M.

I take the letter to Michael's apartment building and go up on the roof where we used to hang out at night, smoking cigarettes and sometimes listening to music. So many summer nights, us up there, away from everything, like we were the only people in the whole city. Now it's so friggin' cold I can even see the air coming out of my nose when I breathe, like I'm some kind of dragon. I light a joint and sit on the roof ledge by the stairwell door, taking shelter from the freezing wind.

It's dark. Late. About eleven o'clock. The city is resting quietly below, under a light, new snowfall.

His building is close to the airport, so all the roofs have red lights flashing and pulsing up long antennas. Michael used to say they were urban shooting stars and that meant you could make a hundred wishes a night if you wanted to. I look at them now without interest. I'm so tired of wishes.

A plane jets by overheard, shaking the air. I can smell the gas vapours.

With frozen fingers, I take the letter out of my pocket. I can't decide if I should burn it or tear it into little pieces or just crumple it into a ball and let it fly away in the wind. I sit there a while longer and smoke another joint. I make myself go over, for the last time, all our experiences together. I think of Michael's face and his hands and his voice and the way he looked at me and his kindness … and I so don't want to let it all go. My tears are so heavy and slow I wonder if it's possible they can freeze on my cheeks.

After some time, my bum turns numb from sitting so long on the cold concrete ledge. Then Ally calls.

"Yo. Mel. You wanna come over?"

"Where?"

"Just chillin' at Devon's with Jess. Watching a flick. Nothing big. But we have juice."

I actually think about it for a second. It's a while that I've been out of the hospital now. I'd love a few drinks. And it *is* Friday night. I shouldn't go. What about all that time and effort I've put into changing my life? Part of me feels like the new me is delusional. Some kind of out-of-body experience. Like I was abducted from my life for a while only to be plopped back down in the centre of it, now, here on the roof, with Ally on the phone. It's like, "Fuck it, who was I kidding?" People can't change everything about them just like that. Sometimes you just have to accept that you're not going to be the perfect person everyone else seems to be.

"Nah." The word comes out of my mouth before I even realize I'm turning her down. I can't believe it! It's like I'm possessed, 'cause I didn't think it's what I wanted to say.

"Okay. Thought I'd ask," she says, letting me off the hook too easy. "Later."

And then she hangs up.

I'm stunned for a second. I can't believe I just said no. I can't believe she just let me. And the thing is, I feel like I'm not really missing much anyway. I'm not that disappointed. I'm just as happy, for now, to go home and watch boring TV.

I jump down off the ledge, raise the letter to my mouth, and kiss it. "Goodbye, Michael," I say. Then I tear the paper up into little pieces, open my fist to the wind, and watch them spastically flutter downward like amputated dove wings.

Sixty-One

My mom and I go to the mall on Saturday afternoon to buy her a new pair of jeans and something for me for Christmas. Even though she's over three months, she barely shows. She refuses to go to the maternity store and get those elastic trousers, and so we search Old Navy for jeans that will fit her belly but are two sizes too big for her legs. We share a change room and we contemplate each other's choices while posing in the mirror. It makes me feel good to see my mom fatter now. It makes me feel less clunky.

"Eric told me I had to tell you something," I say while I'm slipping one leg into a pair of cargo pants. I'm about to tell her about our conversation about Bradley. At first I didn't think I'd ever be saying anything, but lately I've been thinking more and more about it, and I think that maybe there *is* something eating away at the inside of me. I figure if I've gone this far with the truth, I might as well cross the finish line. No more Echo. Now it's only "Melissa" with my mom.

"What's that, Hon?" She reaches out to straighten the collar of the blouse I'm trying on. "Wait, there's something wrong with this button. There, that's better."

My heart races. I don't know why I'm so nervous. It's just words.

Up, up, up.

"It's kind of dumb. But he's making me say it," I say, which is a total lie because Eric said only if I felt up to it.

"Okay."

"He wants me to tell you that I have some bad feelings about Bradley dying."

She puts her hands down and steps away a bit. I realize I'm totally hitting her out of the blue with this. I regret having brought it up now, especially when we're squeezed inside this tiny closet of a room. There is nowhere to hide.

"Oh ... I can understand that. What kind of feelings?"

"Well. It's like ... I'm sad he died. For sure. And I love him. But since I was a kid, and I had kid feelings at the time, I guess I felt sort of angry."

"At me?"

"Yeah. At you," I agree too quickly. I was trying to tell her about Bradley, but it's so much easier talking about being mad at her. "'Cause we had to go in a shelter. Even though I know, now, that it wasn't your fault. It's like the kid in me already made the memory."

"I'm sorry, Melissa. I really tried my best. That's why we went to the shelter—to stay together. They advised me to go to the hospital, but I insisted on outpatient care. I couldn't leave you."

"Yeah. Well ..." I pause. I can't say the words. My mouth is dry. I try to swallow. I don't look at her face, but instead concentrate on the back of her head reflected in one of the angled mirrors. "... I was also mad at Bradley."

"You were?" she asks, surprised.

"Yeah. For dying."

"Oh ..."

"Well. I didn't think so before ... I mean, it wasn't on my mind," I interrupt her before she can respond, "but now that I think about it, maybe I was. I told you it was dumb."

"Oh, Hon. It's not dumb. It's just life. God, if you knew my feelings, you'd understand the real meaning of dumb. Don't worry. I get it. And I'm sorry you had to go through all of that."

"It's okay," I breathe out heavily, as if I've been holding it for the past four years.

She smiles and holds out her arms to hug me. So much hugging lately. I roll my eyes and move into her embrace. It feels so stupid. Like some stupid Christian TV family drama. After a few seconds she pulls away. "So you're cured, then? No more charges? Fights? A's in school from now on?" She laughs and playfully pushes my shoulder.

"Ha ha," I say, and push her back, just a little harder. "What do you think of these?" I ask, turning around and pushing my bum out to show her the cargo pants.

"Perfect."

And it's like nothing and everything has changed between us.

Sixty-Two

As much as you might want to leave your life, just step out of it for a while and hide, it finds you. It sneaks through the window, over the phone, or even walks straight in the front door.

I'm watching the old show *Rudolph the Red-Nosed Reindeer* when Giovanni opens the apartment door and enters the living room. I'm wearing a tank top with no bra and my short shorts because the building's heat is so friggin' strong that we have to keep our windows open in the middle of winter. Seeing Giovanni is my biggest nightmare. I've managed to avoid him until now. The sight of him makes me sick. I think he feels the same, because when he sees me, he stops and stares wide-eyed, like he's shocked I'm here.

"Where's Janet?" he asks.

"Out."

He pauses, like he's considering whether to say something to me or not. Like he's thinking about fucking me. And I get scared. My stomach churns. I can't breathe. I instinctively reach for the blanket to cover up my body, but then I stop myself 'cause I don't want him to think I'm scared. And if what happened between us before is what saved us from getting evicted, then I'd have no choice but to do it again.

He picks up our pile of mail on the table beside him and looks through it, like he's really interested in it. But I can tell he's just killing time. Building courage. I try to watch the TV, but I can't. The tension is too much. I want to get it over with.

"So, you want to do it?" I ask. I don't know why I said it. 'Cause he expects it? 'Cause I don't want us to lose the apartment? It's like the words just ran out of my mouth. Suddenly I'm not Melissa. Suddenly I'm some other person who'll do whatever she must to get what she needs. I reach up behind my head. I try to look sexy, as sexy as possible without throwing up. I do this and I just don't know why.

His mouth drops. He looks angry. Then he looks away. I'm surprised. Something's wrong. I sit up a bit and grab the blanket to cover myself. He looks over his shoulder, as if checking to make sure no one is around, then slowly approaches.

I get nervous. He looks too serious. My heart beats a million times a minute. I feel like I need to put something between us, block him. With what? Words? "Thanks for helping my mom," I blurt out, referring to him not throwing us out.

He stops a few feet away and sits down on the coffee table. I relax a bit. He puts his hands on his knees and sighs deeply. "Melissa. This is a terrible situation. I feel awful about it. You're a young woman. My niece's age. I don't know what happened."

I avert my eyes from his now gentle stare. "I was messed up on drugs. I barely even remember," I say.

"You're sixteen?"

I nod my head, suddenly feeling like a child and not the sexy woman I thought he wanted to fuck. I don't know what to say. I feel totally embarrassed now. I pull the blanket up to my chin. Then I bring my hand up to cover my eyes, because I just want him to disappear. I think of what Eric told me, about experiences being like seeds planted inside you. Maybe my plan of recording over the memory of what happened with Giovanni with a recollection of Bradley will only bury the experience deeper, to grow stronger later.

He clears his throat.

Silence.

"I feel sick about it. Just sick. So sick," he continues.

Leave. Leave. Leave.

He clears his throat again. Silence.

Big sigh. Cough. He clears his throat again. "I'm going to help you and your mom not because of what happened, but *because* of what happened ..."

Shut up. Shut up. Shut up.

"Okay? You get it?"

"No," I say, both hands covering my eyes now.

Leave. Leave. Leave.

"Let's forget it ever happened. And don't tell anyone. Especially your ma. Ever. Okay?"

"Yeah," I reply, and pull the blanket up over my face. And suddenly I *am* only sixteen.

Sixty-Three

Crystal comes over the next afternoon. She has her own key. God, does everybody feel free to just walk into our apartment?

As usual, I'm reading a book and watching a movie at the same time. Other than going to school, it's all I've been doing lately.

"She's not here," I say when she appears in the living room doorway. I don't even raise my eyes from the page.

"Oh, I'm not here to see your mom," she announces, waltzing into the room. The shimmering silver Christmas star earrings she's wearing catch the TV glare. Her big tits sway under her baggy blue T-shirt. I wish she'd wear a bra. "I'm here to see you!" She plops down beside me, too close, and then plunks a pink satin satchel down on the coffee table. I now keep my eyes locked on the TV screen; I don't like her forcing all that huru-guru hippie stuff on me. She raises the converter and turns it off. Then she leans over and carefully unties the purple string, as if she's about to reveal diamonds, only she ends up spilling out a bunch of blue and green rocks.

I eye them quickly, pretending not to notice how pretty they are. I don't want to give her the satisfaction.

248 LESLEY ANNE COWAN

"I brought you these to revitalize your energy," she says, all perky. She gingerly picks up each stone with her skinny fingers and holds it up in front of my face, blocking my view. "This one is to help with your spirit. This one will help with appetite. This one is for nourishing the starving soul. And this one is to soothe your sexual goddess."

"Huh?" I look at her for the first time. "My what?"

She smiles that stupid smug smile, like she's won. "Your sexual goddess within. We are all sexual goddesses, Melissa. Sometimes we women forget that—God knows I must remind your mother all the time—but we are all goddesses of the earth."

"And they think *I'm* crazy," I say, holding my hand out to take the stone.

"Mel, it's none of my business—"

"You're right, it's not your business," I interrupt her, because she has no right sticking her nose in my life.

She pouts. "But you don't even know what I'm gonna say."

I shrug my shoulders. I couldn't care less.

"Well, I'm going to say it anyway. And I'm going to say it straight out. Sexual relations, Melissa, are a gift in life."

"Oh, God …" I turn away as if her statement is making me sick.

"Hear me out, Mel. There's a lot of crap and suffering in life, but sexual contact is a gift. It's something that can be really beautiful and special. I'm not talking about saving yourself for marriage. Even a one-night encounter with someone you find irresistible can be gratifying. Ha!" Her voice starts to wander. "I've had some beautifully erotic encounters on foreign beaches under a full moon that—"

"Okay!" I interrupt again, holding my hand up to indicate *stop*. It's just disgusting to hear old people talk about sex.

"Anyway. You get what I mean. The important thing is the connection between two people. If you reduce sex to something as common as a handshake, then you're missing out on that connection. People need to connect to other people, Melissa. It's something integral to your soul. And you need to feed your soul, Mel. Feed it, or it will die. You will die inside. You will be empty."

I pretend I'm not listening, but I am. Because what she's saying sort of makes sense. And if it weren't for me being with Michael, feeling how special that was, I don't think I would ever have come close to understanding her point.

"Tell me, Mel. Why do you think you give your body away so freely, while you hold on to your words, your feelings, so tightly? It seems to me it should be the other way around. Shouldn't it? You're a teenager. You need to talk about how you feel."

"Oh, God …" I hide my face in the couch cushion. I can't take the awkwardness.

Relentless, she leans in and takes my hands in hers. "Your body is sacred, Melissa. Your body is beautiful and miraculous and sacred."

I feel like an idiot sitting here on the couch holding hands. But I let her continue because otherwise she'll keep pestering me.

"Your body is sacred. It's the most miraculous thing you own. Can you say you truly own anything, Melissa? Anything except your own body? A woman's body is the most precious gift. If you give it away for free, it becomes worthless. And then the most precious, the most valuable thing you own, your body, becomes worthless. And soon you begin to feel worthless as well."

She flips over my right hand and starts to rub my palm.

"Do you feel worthless, Melissa?"

Her question freaks me out. It's a terrible thing to ask. Not many things people say can truly shock me. But for once, an adult, this crazy lady, is speaking the truth. For once, someone has had the guts to say it like it is. I'm both excited and upset: excited because I finally have an answer but upset at the bare-boned truth. Do I feel worthless?

Yes. That is exactly how I feel. *Worthless.*

And every guy I was with, every fuckin' one of them, has stripped my soul. How did I not see that?

She doesn't wait for me to answer. "Your body is sacred," she repeats.

"You said that already."

"Your body is sacred," she says again, like she didn't even hear me. She just keeps rubbing my palm.

"Okay ... enough." I pull my hand away a bit, but she holds tight and keeps rubbing, so I just let her do what she wants.

"Your body is sacred. Your body is sacred," she says again and again, as if she were chanting, her eyes closed. My palm starts to burn. I feel so dumb, but for some reason I don't really want to stop her, so I close my eyes so I don't feel as stupid.

"My body is sacred, my body is sacred, my body is sacred ..." she starts chanting, over and over, so that the words, the rhythm, start to go into my head. And I find myself thinking the words along with her, and they don't sound so dumb anymore.

My body is sacred. My body is sacred. My body is sacred.

Sixty-Four

Fortune calls my cell at two in the morning. He's called me lots of times in the past couple of weeks, but I never answer. This time I do, because I'm still awake. He tells me he wants to see me. He pretends nothing ever happened between us, that there was no fight. He doesn't even ask me about my OD, though I'm sure he knows. He just picks up the conversation like we were hanging out only yesterday.

"I'm doing my own thing," I say groggily.

"What's that mean?"

"I mean, I'm on my own. I don't want a boyfriend. I'm gonna be alone."

"Ha! *You* can't be alone."

"Fuck you," I say, in a joking way. I have to admit, it feels sort of nice to be talking to him.

"Come on, baby, come over." His voice sounds quiet and sleepy and sexy. "I wanna see you. I wanna hold you, babe. I miss you so much ..."

I pull my blanket over my head. "You don't miss me."

"I do. Really. I think about you all the time. I miss your body—"

"My body is sacred," I interrupt him before I can stop the words from coming out of my mouth.

He laughs. "Wha'd you say?"

"Forget it."

He starts laughing really hard. "Did you say your body is *sacred*?" Then he starts fake-laughing just to make me feel like an idiot. And I wonder, why was I ever into him in the first place? At first I think about explaining my words, telling him about Crystal and what happened, but then I think it's just too long a story and he won't get it, and why do I need to explain anything to him anyway? I'll prove to him, to everyone, that I changed just by living my life. He'll see that I'm not messing around with guys anymore. He'll see that soon enough.

"Whatever. I gotta go." I close the phone and switch it off.

Freestyle told me, "Never try to teach a pig to think. It doesn't work, and it annoys the pig."

Sixty-Five

I've realized something these past few weeks, since the hospital. My mind is now clear and ideas are coming so easily. I'm beginning to think that when you're in a relationship, it's not about how beautiful the other person looks, it's about how beautiful you become when you're with them. With Michael I was beautiful, inside and out. I said the right things. I did the right things. I liked who I was.

And I have been thinking that maybe I've been Echo *all* the time—in my home, my neighbourhood, with friends. It's not just with adults. It's *always*. And maybe it's not just the words I've been reflecting back to everyone. Maybe it's also the ugliness. And the hate. And the fear. And the anger. And the self-loathing.

A while ago I remember believing that I was simply reflecting Michael's beauty. But now, when I really, really think about it, perhaps because he was so calm and clear, quite possibly Michael was reflecting mine.

Up. Up. Up.

Sixty-Six

I am sleeping soundly the night before my court date when shouting from the living room wakes me up. A man's voice. Someone I don't recognize. And my mom's high, screechy voice. They are both yelling in the living room, but I can't really make out a lot other than swearing. It gets bad. And then it gets really ugly. I hear a fist in his voice. I've heard it before, in other men's voices. It's why I keep a baseball bat behind my dresser. All these thoughts and images go through my mind. My bloodied mother, dead on the floor. The man coming into my room to finish the job.

I rip open my door. They both turn to me. "Melissa!" my mom shouts, horrified because I'm holding the bat over my shoulder.

"Get out of here!" I shout, storming toward the middle-aged, muscle-headed man with a ball cap and a goatee.

He holds up his hands like he's surrendering. "Hey, hey ... take it easy, Honey ..."

"Melissa!" my mom shouts. "Stop! Put it down."

"Who the fuck are you?" I insist, still on the attack.

Wham. Black. Black. Throbbing in my ears. Then ringing.

My face pains. I can't see. Then little bits of light come into my eyes. Then little bits more. And I start to make out the guy standing in front of me, but I look harder and I see it's my mother.

My mother hit me!

"You fucking hit me …"

"Melissa! Melissa!" she shouts, shaking my shoulders.

"What the fuck? You fucking hit me?" I keep shouting, because I just can't believe it happened.

"Melissa! Melissa! Look at me. Are you crazy? What are you going to do with the bat?" Her voice trembles.

I look over her shoulder and around the room for the guy. "Where is he?" My hands are still gripping the bat. My fists get tighter. I'm ready to use it.

I feel her hands on my hands. She pushes the bat down. "He's gone, Melissa. He took off when he saw you."

"You hit me?" I question her again, still a little out of it.

"I'm sorry, Hon." She reaches out a hand to stroke my cheek.

"Ow!" I pull away at her painful touch.

She reaches her hand back out and with a finger gently dabs just under my eye. "You're bleeding. It was my ring. Oh God, I'm sorry." She pulls me into her. My arms reflexively go around her back, but I'm still holding the stupid baseball bat. I won't let it go.

"Is the door locked?" I ask, pushing her away. Without waiting for an answer, I go through the kitchen, bolt the door, and put the chain on. "Who was that? What if he comes back?" I scream.

"I'm calling Giovanni." My mom heads toward the phone.

"No! Don't!" There's panic in my voice. Too much panic.

She turns and looks at me inquisitively. "Why not? What's *wrong* with you lately?"

"Just don't. We don't need him. You'll wake him up."

She lifts up the receiver. "He'll understand. He'll come stay on the couch."

She breaks down crying when she talks to Giovanni on the phone. I know he'll be up in a few seconds. I leave the room to inspect my eye in the washroom mirror. The cut's not deep, but I'm already puffy. So I get some ice from the kitchen, wrap it in a tea towel, and then go into my room. I sit down, my back against the door, head in hands, and wait. Wait. And I hear Giovanni come in through the kitchen. I hear my mom crying. I hear his murmuring for a long time. Then I hear them both walk through the living room. I hear two sets of feet pass. I hear her bedroom door shut. I feel sick to my stomach.

I lie with my face pressed against the dusty hardwood floor. I just can't believe it happened. This night. That man. My mother hitting me. Just when things were getting better, things got worse. I want to cry, but my eye hurts too much and I'm all dried up anyway.

Sixty-Seven

The sound of the phone ringing in the kitchen wakes me up the next morning. I'm still lying on the floor. I hear footsteps then a gentle knock at my door. "Melissa? That was Sue who called. We need to be there by eleven."

"Where?" I ask groggily. I can't make things out clearly anymore.

"Court. Remember?"

I forgot. I'm supposed to go to court today. I'm supposed to stand before a judge and say how great my life is going, that I've turned things around. I'm not supposed to tell him that I almost killed a stranger with a baseball bat last night.

I peek out to the living room. My mother's bedroom door is open. There's no sign of Giovanni or his shoes or his tool belt or his smell. In the washroom, I stand staring at my face in the mirror, my stupid fucking face. Will my life ever really change? Trouble seems to find me even in my sleep. I try not to feel sorry for myself, because feeling sorry for yourself gets you nowhere. And in some ways I feel good, because I stood up for me and my mom and I'm strong and I'm going to go far in life. I'm going to get out of the fucking boat if it's the last thing I do.

"We'll put some makeup on it. You won't even be able to tell," my mom says, squeezing into the washroom. She bends down and takes a shoebox full of old makeup out from under the sink. "Sit on the toilet seat and let me do my magic. I know a thing or two about this."

I don't say anything but just do what she tells me. I'm sort of mad at her for bringing that guy around. I thought things had changed. Then I think of her and Giovanni together while I stare at her rounded belly in front of my face.

"I'm so sorry about last night," she says.

"Who was he?"

"Ahh." She waves her hand in the air. "It was stupid. Some guy from the tavern. I shouldn't have brought him home. He seemed okay, but once he saw my belly, he got real angry."

"You shouldn't bring strange men back here. We'll end up dead."

"I know," she says. "I'm sorry. Sometimes I'm so stupid."

"Yeah, you are," I agree.

She swats me gently on the shoulder as if she's completely offended, but laughs immediately afterward. "We'll get through this, Hon," she says, and kisses me on the tip of my nose. "Let's take one day at a time. Let's get through this court day."

Sixty-Eight

I sit between my mother and my social worker, Sue, on the bench outside the courtroom, waiting for them to call my case number.

Sue hasn't commented yet on my bruised face, but this close up she must see it. I figure she thinks some guy is messing me up and she'll ask me about it later. Meanwhile, she and my mom make small talk. I can tell my mom is trying her best to avoid the issue of my black eye by bombarding Sue with question after question, about nothing important.

I stop listening to them, lean back into the bench, and close my eyes. I'm so tired from last night that all I want to do is sleep. It's crazy how calm I feel. I'm not even worried about what the judge will say. If I go to jail, then I'll get out of my house for a while. If I don't get convicted, then I'll think again about moving into that group home. It's that simple.

My head starts to bob up and down. But instead of sleeping, this instantaneous flash of my life happens, the way they say it does before you die. Everything all at once, yet played out in detail. It's like my entire sixteen years are captured in a moment. Then I jerk up my head, the way you do after you dream you're falling.

And for a second, a split second, maybe just a millithousandth of a second, I feel like everything that's happened to me has been worth it. Like somehow, next time, I'll know just a little more, get closer to doing the right thing, saying the right thing. I'm proud of the changes I've made, even if they are small. Maybe I'm not doomed like Sisyphus. Sure, I will roll the rock up and down, but there will be a summit. An end. And my arms will be that much stronger from all that pushing and chasing.

I feel a hand grip my knee and am startled out of my dozing. "That's us! You're lucky that Rachel didn't call the police about the property assault," Sue says, tapping me gently on the thigh. "Don't worry. It's likely they'll drop the break-and-enter charge. You've got a good judge."

Sixty-Nine

The judge is a kind-looking old man with greying hair and laugh lines around his eyes. He sort of reminds me of Anthony Hopkins—when he played a quiet butler in a movie, not when he was Hannibal Lecter. After a while of blah blah blah to no one in particular, he finally directs a question to me. "Well, Melissa. It's been three months. You've had a chance to reflect on your actions. I see you've been going to counselling regularly and you're passing your courses. I know there was some recent trouble, but I'm assured you have good supports in place. I have your latest report card here in my hand. Good grades …"

As he's talking, I stare him down with my black eye that's no doubt revealed itself under the pasty foundation diluted by sweat. I keep staring, letting him get a good look at me, wanting him to notice the cracks in my face, the way Ms. Dally did, because in a way I still want someone to fix me. To give me another chance. Send me somewhere else, away from everyone I know.

I wait and wait. Staring. I do it long enough for it to become awkward. But he seems clueless. He just goes on about the consequences of my actions being a chain effect, and how it's often the parents, the mothers, who bear the stress of a teen who just can't make things work …

"Do you know what you want to do when you graduate from high school?" he asks.

My mom takes my hand and squeezes tightly, cueing me to respond, to say the right thing.

"When I graduate from high school? A veterinarian," Echo says, which is the right answer, because he smiles at both me and my mom and relaxes in his chair.

"How wonderful."

⟶

I take it back. Kids are not the only ones who see only black and white. Adults do too. I think there's this phase as a teenager where things are murky, when the truth is naked and raw. You see people wholly. You see all the hypocrisy and the contradictions, the intertwined good and bad. But it's so stressful and confusing to see things this way that eventually you stop looking. The little window of perception closes up and you learn to keep it shut. You jam it with something so it doesn't open up again. And just like that, people are put back into their blacks and whites, a little more categorized, but clearly divided all the same.

Then you get older and you forget that you are seeing only one side of people. I suppose it's easier to go through life that way. But if you really stopped to think about it, you would understand the jerk who pushes you out of the way, or the bitch in the coffee shop lineup who sighs and mutters about the noisy kid, or the punk who keys your car … You'd know there's something behind that behaviour. But you don't care.

It's too late, because you've learned to be an echo for so long that even you have forgotten who you used to be.

"So tell me, Melissa, how things are going. Better?" the judge continues, his hopeful eyes awaiting my response.

I feel my heart pound in my chest. What is the right answer? So maybe I'm not doomed to be Sisyphus, but I'm not quite ready to completely let go of Echo yet. I don't know if I ever will be. Freestyle says, "You can't change the system. Never try. It's a machine that will keep running with or without you. Stick a wrench in it and the interruption is only temporary. It will rev up again and you'll just be left tired and without a wrench."

Up. Up. Up.

"Better," Echo repeats, and forces her best smile.